BREATHE

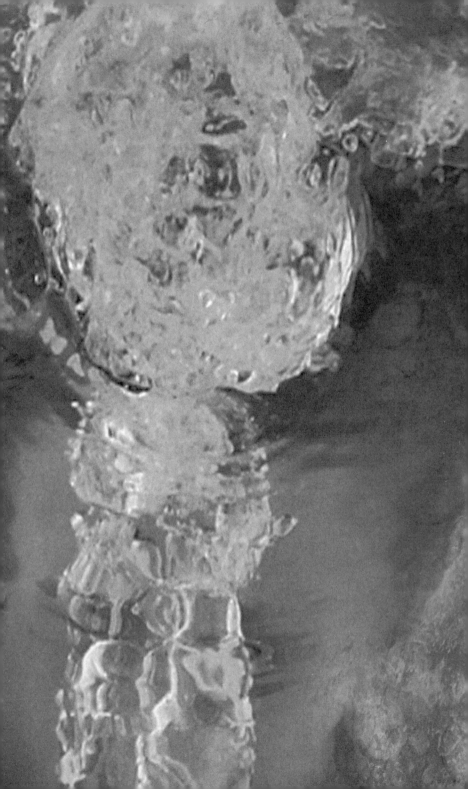

BREATHE

PENNI RUSSON

GREENWILLOW BOOKS
An Imprint of HarperCollinsPublishers

Breathe
Copyright © 2005 by Penni Russon
First published in 2005 in Australia
by Random House Australia.
First published in 2007 in the United States
by Greenwillow Books.
All rights reserved. No part of this book may be used or
reproduced in any manner whatsoever without written per-
mission except in the case of brief quotations embodied in
critical articles and reviews. Printed in the United States of
America. For information address HarperCollins Children's
Books, a division of HarperCollins Publishers, 1350
Avenue of the Americas, New York, NY 10019.
www.harpercollinschildrens.com

The text of this book is set in Adobe Caslon.
Book design by Chad W. Beckerman.

Library of Congress Cataloging-in-Publication Data
Russon, Penni.
Breathe / by Penni Russon.
p. cm.
"Greenwillow Books."
Sequel to: Undine.
Summary: Undine is excited about leaving Tasmania for a trip
to see her father in Greece but conflicted about using the magic
that wells up inside her and confused about her personal
relationships, including the one with her best friend, Trout.
ISBN-13: 978-0-06-079393-7 (trade bdg.)
ISBN-10: 0-06-079393-7 (trade bdg.)
ISBN-13: 978-0-06-079394-4 (lib. bdg.)
ISBN-10: 0-06-079394-5 (lib. bdg.)
[1. Magic—Fiction. 2. Interpersonal relationships—Fiction.
3. Conduct of life—Fiction. 4. Tasmania—Fiction.
5. Australia—Fiction. 6. Greece—Fiction.] I. Title.
PZ7.R9194Bre 2007 [Fic]—dc22 2006000944

First American Edition 10 9 8 7 6 5 4 3 2 1

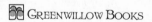 GREENWILLOW BOOKS

FOR MUM, DAD, AND KYLIE,
THANKS FOR GIVING ME STORIES

AND FOR CAROLYN AND CHRISTOPHER,
A STORY COME TRUE

PROLOGUE

The first time, it is late summer. The days are drawing in. Every night the dark comes like the tide: inevitably. He tries to hold it back, he clenches his mind like a fist against it, but the dark comes anyway.

The house shifts and settles, but its occupants are silent. All the world is sleeping, except Trout. He lies awake, but sleeplessness isn't the problem. It's the dream, every night the same, vivid and relentless.

Tonight he doesn't wait for it. He gets dressed. He pads down the stairs, his feet light and soft as big cats' paws. He eases the front door open and closed. Outside, red bricks and asphalt hold the heat of the day, but the air is light and fresh and smells of change. He walks toward the city.

He has this thought, that he is the only person left in the world. That he is walking through an abandoned streetscape and will find every building deserted, every human heart expired. Even the stars seem cool and distant. So it is a relief when he sees, at the dark end of a small street, an old man urinating into the gutter.

He takes comfort in the company of strangers: cleaners, night nurses, bakers, and security guards; thieves and vandals and runaways; the drunk and dispossessed; the lonely, the lost, and the angry. He imagines himself a protector of sorts, a witness. He is privy to the city's secrets.

In the day he is merely a shadow of his nighttime self. When sunlight illuminates the darkness within him, he fears the dark. But here, in the night, there is no fear. His future lies waiting in the city's black heart. The night has plans for them all.

Part One

TROUT

CHAPTER ONE

From her bedroom window, Undine could see the top of Mount Wellington, iced stingily with a narrow sliver of snow. Down on the street Trout's brother Dan lovingly poured water on his brown Datsun, sealed in a thin veneer of frost. Steam clouded upward into the brittle air.

She bent down and folded, then unfolded, the cuff of her jeans. Year Twelve, and the only difference she could see was that they were allowed to wear what they liked. Well, not the only difference, though school had little to do with her personal transformation.

She stood at the window, watching for Trout.

"Undine!" Lou called up the stairs. "You'll miss the bus."

Downstairs Jasper was wearing his rainbow gumboots and nothing else. He waved his toothbrush.

"Don't you think he looks a little . . . fruity?" Undine asked.

Lou laughed. "Come here, you," she said, but Jasper took off squealing, his boots clomping on the wooden floor.

Undine watched his bare bottom disappear through his bedroom door. "Gotta go!" she said to Lou, heading for the front door.

"Wait!" Lou called. She tossed Undine an apple and a banana from the wooden bowl on the kitchen table.

Undine looked down at the fruit in her hands with faint derision. "Nice parenting, Lou."

"Wait," said Lou again, more seriously this time. "Let me look at you."

Undine rolled her eyes and spread out her arms and tilted her face back. "Go on, then."

Lou came over. She put both hands on Undine's

cheeks and scrutinized Undine's face with careful attention. "How are you feeling?" she asked.

"Fine," said Undine.

"Anything happening?"

"Look, it's under control. I love that you care, but you don't have to do this. I really will miss the bus."

Lou's eyes held Undine's for an extra moment. "Okay, chickadee," she said finally, kissing Undine's forehead. "Is Dominic coming for dinner tonight?"

"I don't know."

The front door banged behind her, and Undine stood for a moment on the other side of it. She hadn't been exactly lying to Lou; she did have it under control, but only just.

Breathe-in-two-three-out-two-three . . . She focused her mind and held it in, that extraordinary power, that darkness: the magic.

Trout woke, wearing last night's clothes. His head ached; his neck was stiff and sore. He rolled over and looked at the clock. He would miss the bus. He closed his eyes again.

For the second time in a week, Trout hadn't done his homework. A year ago, Trout wouldn't have known who he was if he had missed a single assignment. He was diligent with schoolwork, he studied astronomy and read Shakespeare in his own time, he sat in on the occasional university lecture in his free periods . . . he could even recite pi to seventy-two places. He was neither popular nor unpopular; he was liked well enough in a nerdy kind of way.

Yep, a year ago, Trout had known exactly who he was, and by far the most important thing about him, his most distinguishing feature, the thing that dominated his unspectacular universe, was a girl: Undine Louise Connelly, the girl next door. They had been best friends. They still were, he supposed, officially anyway.

She had not loved him, but he had loved her, and for years that had been enough, that unrequited, familiar, slightly excruciating but not especially risky love.

But now it was all different. Oh, he still loved her. But it ate him daily, that love, leaving less and less of him behind. Where he had once been whole, he was now damaged, exposed parts. He loved her, but sometimes he hated her for it.

Someone knocked on his door. He pulled the duvet up to his chin to hide his crumpled clothes.

"I'm up," he called, his voice muffled.

"Yeah, right." It was Dan. He stood in the doorway, jangling his car keys.

Trout groaned. "What gave me away?"

"How about seventeen years of undeniable history?"

"Grumble."

"And they say you're the smart one. I suppose you want another lift?"

"Come on, you love it. Any excuse to drive that clapped-out demon of yours."

Dan backed out of the room. "You take that back or you'll be walking to school. That's a *lady* you're talking about."

Trout rubbed his eyes and forced himself to get

up. He drew back his curtain to check the day. Day cold. Big surprise.

Undine was standing outside her front door. A wave of tiredness came over him.

She looked so forlorn, standing there, and he felt suddenly sorry for her, uncomplicated by any other feelings. But then those other feelings intruded; the raw, injured parts of him began to throb, and the moment was gone.

Undine lingered outside the door to Trout's house, but didn't go in.

For the last seven years or so, Undine had met Trout every morning before school at his house, hurrying him along so he wouldn't miss the bus. However, from the beginning of this school year, Trout had been ready and waiting for her at the bottom of the stepped laneway to Undine's house.

Then one day, Trout hadn't been there at all. When Undine had knocked on the side door, Mrs.

M. coolly informed her that Trout had left for school. He was at the bus stop already, talking to a couple of Year Eleven boys, and had hardly looked up when she joined them. Now he didn't seem to catch the bus anymore.

Undine had always taken Trout's feelings for her for granted. No, she hadn't; she had *wished them away* more times than she could count, and with desperate fervor. Well, now it seemed she was getting her wish: Trout was going off her. It didn't feel good, now that it had happened. She modified her wishing, but she feared it was too late. She didn't want his feelings for her to be messy, spilling over into romance. But she wanted them to be friends again, *best* friends, not these two awkward almost-strangers.

"When did we stop talking to each other?" she asked the wintry air. Of course, they still talked. But there was so much unmentioned, every conversation was a minefield. Undine couldn't pinpoint how certain topics had become taboo. She had once told Trout

7

everything. Now they talked about nothing—filling the heavy silence between them with lightweight, inadequate words that tumbled through the air away from them.

As she'd expected, Trout wasn't at the bus stop. She sat in the shelter and waited, the absence of Trout a ragged hole inside her.

CHAPTER TWO

The school day rolled by, unremarkable. Trout arrived; she watched from the window of her top floor classroom as he walked down the school driveway, five minutes late but in no hurry. At lunchtime she caught him outside the library.

"Trout, I—"

For a moment it seemed he might stop, but then Dominic appeared from nowhere, his arm sliding around her shoulders.

"G'day, Montmorency," Dominic said, affably enough, to Trout.

Trout smiled vaguely. "Gotta run," he said, tapping

his wrist, though he wasn't wearing a watch. "See you on the bus after school."

Undine watched Trout go; Dominic twisted his finger in her hair.

Later, as Undine got on the bus, she saw Trout through the crowd of students jostling for the several buses that queued in the school's driveway. He looked straight through her, as if she were made of glass.

He climbed on a different bus from hers, one heading for the city. Without Trout's company, the trip seemed interminably long, the crowded bus stuffy and overheated. Undine didn't get a seat and stood in the aisle, buffeted by the lurching motion of the bus.

There was a letter waiting for Undine when she got home. There was also one for Lou, with the same handwriting on the envelope. Undine was far more curious about Lou's letter than her own, though she opened the one addressed to herself and read it standing just inside the door.

Beach Road

Bay of Angels

Dear Undine,

As I write, Flopsy and Mopsy chase insects outside, batting their paws against the windowpanes. Cottontail and Peter fight in the hallway, stalking each other's long tails. Mother cat still refuses to come in, but I am working on her . . . this morning she drank some milk from a bowl just inside the back door. As a thank you, she left a rat on the step. That kind of gratitude I can live without. Ariel is groaning doggily in her sleep; perhaps she is dreaming of a past day, when she was queen of her domain, and there were no blasted cats.

You haven't seen the bay in winter yet: the sea is wilder now. The angels are buffeted by the wind and waves, ground by salt and sand, but still they stand, rigidly holy, bearing witness to the tide.

Did you know that Alastair and his university cronies will be diving the wreck in August? I have given them permission to use my land. Alastair will live in the house

and care for the animals. I will be heading for warmer
climes for the duration.

Best,
Prospero

It was a fairly typical letter from her father, with little outward sentiment. He did not mention the magic, at her request. She had told him she would not be using it and that she would not discuss it. He had protested, but faintly, diminished by his shame.

She read the letter again, skittering over the references to Alastair—she wasn't ready to think about him again. What did Prospero mean by warmer climes? She couldn't imagine her elderly father in shorts and a T-shirt on the Gold Coast, with a beer in his hand and zinc cream on his nose.

Undine was in the middle of homework when Lou and Jasper came home. Jasper went straight into his room and emerged moments later, stripped bare, wearing his rainbow boots and carrying his beloved toothbrush. He scavenged a cookie and headed into his corner of the lounge room, where his blocks and toys were kept, and set about with absorbed industry.

"You've got a letter," Undine told Lou.

Lou picked it up and turned it over a few times in her hands. "What does *he* want?" she asked suspiciously.

"Well, I doubt it's triggered to explode," Undine teased. "Go on. Open it."

"I will if you make me a cup of coffee," bargained Lou.

As the kettle came to a boil, Lou exclaimed out loud, "No! Absolutely not! Over my dead body."

Undine hurtled from the kitchen. "What?"

"What did he say to you? Did you know about this? Oh, Undine. I can't believe you would . . ."

"Unless it's something to do with kittens, I know nothing about it. What?"

"He wants you to go *on holiday* with him," Lou choked out. She said it with the same incredulity as if Prospero wanted to take Undine to the moon.

Undine's eyes lit up. She could do with some of

those warmer climes herself. "Really? Cool!"

"No!" said Lou. "Not cool. You are not going. I'm not letting him drag you to the other side of the world, to the armpit of . . ."

"The world?" Undine asked. "Armpit? Where does he want us to go?"

"Doesn't he know how important Year Twelve is? You'd have to take two weeks off school in addition to the term holiday. It's just not practical."

"But I could catch up. I could take work with me," Undine pleaded. "It would be good for me." She picked up Lou's letter, scanning it quickly. "Corfu! Fantastic!"

"He says," Lou said as she flopped back on the couch, "he wants you to discover your roots."

"Roots are good. Family is very important." Undine regarded Lou. Actually, Lou had run away from home when she met Prospero and her family had refused contact with her since, so maybe this wasn't the angle to take. But Lou surprisingly agreed.

"Family *is* important," she said softly. Then she

rallied again. "So is Year Twelve, Undine. Your education has to come first."

"And it will, Lou. I promise. But I really want to go."

Lou took Undine's hands. "Don't you see, my girl? I can't let you go. I can't let you be that far away. I can't let you go with him. We've got a deal, remember?"

"I know. But you can trust me. I wouldn't use the magic, I promise."

"I do trust you," Lou said, but Undine thought she heard a trace of doubt. "I don't trust *him*. And he can be so persuasive, so charismatic . . ."

Later, side by side in the kitchen, Lou assembled a vegetarian lasagne while Undine made a walnut and cheese salad. Undine's mind fizzed as she thought about that captivating word—*Corfu*—but she tried to keep her fizzing to herself.

"Is Dominic coming?" Lou asked.

"I forgot to invite him."

Undine suspected she wasn't a very good girl-friend to Dominic. Dominic seemed to think so;

he complained often of neglect and of the faraway look in Undine's eyes. "No secrets," he had whispered into her neck once, imagining that any secrets they might have would be as harmless as tame mice. Undine had not responded. She had nothing but secrets; she lived with them every day. Big ones and small ones, they wrapped themselves around her heart like lies, and squeezed.

Hearing the sound of Mim's heavy boots clomping up the outside steps, Undine flung open the door before she had a chance to knock. Undine was always glad to see her aunt Mim. She was really a step-aunt, Undine supposed, though she was Jasper's real aunt, but she felt as much Undine's true family as Stephen had.

Mim had Stephen's kind gray eyes, soft and rounded at the edges, and when she smiled at Undine it was as if a part of Stephen had not been lost.

Mim knew a bit about Undine's magic, more than most. She knew that Prospero was Undine's biological father, that he had called to her at night through her dreams, and that his Bay of Angels had magic of its own. She knew that Undine had been able to draw magic from the bay and Prospero had tried to control her, to use her magic for himself. She knew that Trout had tried to save her, and had almost died, but that Prospero had helped her in the end and Lou had come, too, to call her back, away from the magic. But Undine had never told Mim, nor had she let Lou tell her, how close Undine had come to squeezing the life out of the world with her terrifying power.

(Though Undine herself had never been quite clear on that one—when she believed the world to be darkened and contracted into one small grain of light, the rest of the earth's population had apparently been unaware and had gone on eating, sleeping, getting stuck in peak-hour traffic, having sex, disappointing each other, buying houses and toasters and raisins, murdering each other, rescuing each other, writing down each other's phone numbers on the backs of their hands with a ballpoint pen. Even

Mim—Undine had checked—at that precise moment had been gathering white sheets off the line; Undine could see them in her mind's eye: billowing around Mim like sails.)

"Go and get your brother, will you?" Lou asked. "And see if you can persuade him to put something more . . . *suitable* on."

"Suitable?" Mim said. Lou rolled her eyes in her son's direction. Mim saw the rainbow boots and giggled. Lou stared.

"Well," said Mim defensively, "it's pretty cute."

"It *was* pretty cute. It is wearing thin."

Undine went over to the corner. Jasper was arranging his blocks carefully on the ground.

"It's writing," he told her, "but you can only read it if you're on the ceiling." Undine peered up at the white ceiling, relieved to see it was empty. She half expected to see someone spread-eagled on it, reading Jasper's message.

She had often wondered, since she learned that her magic came from Lou, what this meant for

Jasper, whether he had some kind of magic of his own. Sometimes she almost wished he did have it, to share the load. But when she looked at his bright three-year-old face, and Stephen's and Mim's questioning gray eyes that peered out from it, she hoped ardently that he would be free of the magic and all its burdens.

"Is Prospero my daddy, too?" Jasper had once asked out of the blue.

Lou met Undine's eyes. "No, sweetie. He's just Undine's daddy. Your daddy was Stephen, remember?" Lou brought out the photo albums and they looked at photos of Stephen with Undine, with Mim, with Stephen's parents, with familiar family friends, with Lou. In the later photos, Lou's pregnant bump was apparent.

"Where am I?" asked Jasper.

"You weren't born yet, honey. You were in here!" Lou pointed to a photo of her swollen tummy and made her mouth into a widely surprised *o*.

"What's born?" asked Jasper, and so he learned his

first lesson about the birds and the bees: the resilience and frailty of life. He knew death as he had seen it—flies on the windowsill, echidnas and wallabies by the side of the road. But now there was birth, too, and it was astonishing and improbable and Jasper had asked about it many more times, until Lou had finally bought him a book to explain the parts she could not.

Undine reached her hand out. "Come on, little man," she said. "Let's get you dressed for dinner."

Something more suitable turned out to be starry underpants and the top part of his Spider-Man pajamas. Jasper sat up to the table and carefully picked the zucchini and eggplant out of his lasagne.

"Jasper, sweetie," Lou said. "You like eggplant."

He stopped and stared at Lou. "Do I?" He looked at Undine. "*Do* I?" he asked her curiously.

Undine nodded.

"Oh," he said, and continued to pick it out anyway.

"Oh, Jasper," Lou said, exasperated.

"You is cranky," he told Mim. "You doesn't want Undine to go away."

Mim looked confused. Lou explained. "Jasper has picked up Undine's habit of calling me Lou. Except because of his delightful, selective speech impediment, he says *You*. It never fails to confuse people. Including me. And he seems to have no trouble pronouncing the word *lolly*."

"Lol-ly," Jasper said with exaggerated enunciation, by way of demonstration.

Mim waved her hand. "I actually got all that, scarily enough. I spend way too much time with you people. But why would Undine be going away?"

"I had a letter from Undine's father. He wants her to discover her roots."

"But she's not going?"

Lou said nothing, her mouth a stubborn straight line.

"It's just for a few weeks," Undine told Mim plaintively, looking sideways at Lou.

Despite the weight of her disappointment,

Undine couldn't blame Lou. It was to Lou's credit that she let Undine have any kind of relationship with Prospero at all. He had shown no interest in Undine throughout her childhood, only appearing when Undine's powerful talent began to manifest itself. No one, not even Lou, could understand the nuances of Undine's feelings for Prospero. It was complicated and not without twinges of betrayal and mistrust—more than twinges if truth be told—but loving Prospero was apparently an involuntary reflex, something that couldn't be helped.

Undine answered Mim's question. "Lou doesn't really trust Prospero."

Mim looked from Undine to Lou.

"Fair enough."

They ate in silence for a few minutes.

"You know," remarked Mim casually to Lou, looking at her meal. "You could go with them."

Lou's fork froze halfway to her mouth. "I . . . I couldn't."

"You could," said Mim. "If you wanted to."

"Well! What about Jasper?"

"Take him with you."

"And my work?"

"Schedule a break. Come on, Lou. They keep hassling you to have a holiday."

"But Undine's school—"

Undine broke in, flushed with excitement. "Lou, I'm doing so well this year, better than I ever have. If I promise to work really hard . . ."

Lou looked assaulted. "I *couldn't* spend four weeks with that man."

Mim shrugged. "Well, if you *couldn't* . . ." She went back to eating her dinner, but unseen by Lou, Mim gave Undine a big wink.

Lou looked around the table. Undine stared back, brimming with excitement, trying to hold it in. Was Lou caving?

"I . . ." Lou began, pointing her fork in Undine's direction, but did not finish her thought. "We'll see," she said finally.

Undine bounced up and down a little.

"Is that we'll see, *yes*, or we'll see, *no*?"

"It's we'll see, *maybe*," replied Lou. "And *absolutely not* if you keep leaping about like that."

Undine stopped bouncing, but nothing would wipe the smile from her face.

Lou dropped her knife and fork and put her head in her hands. "I must be crazy."

Undine jumped up and hugged Lou, then Mim. "Thank you," she whispered in Mim's ear.

Lou looked at Mim. "This is all your fault, you know."

CHAPTER THREE

Undine skipped down the steps and knocked lightly on Trout's door. Mrs. Montmorency let her in and directed Undine coolly up the stairs to Trout's bedroom. Dan stood at the bottom of the stairs, watching her ascend, his eyes dark and fierce. Undine shivered, glad to get away from both mother and middle son.

She tapped on Trout's bedroom door and, without waiting for a response, flung it open. Trout said, "No!" at the same time. Undine caught her breath, and stood, struck dumb by the sight before her.

It had been months since she'd been in Trout's room. It had always been relatively neat, drab, and functional: bed, desk, chair, bookshelves, and a few childhood leftovers like model boats and a scungy old toy rabbit called Blinks.

The transformation was startling.

Every inch of wall space was covered. On the right, under the heading *Chaos*, there were intricate, symmetrical geometric patterns. On the left, far more disturbing, was the heading *True Chaos*. Here the pictures were distorted, with no discernible pattern or methodology. Sticky notes, scrawled with comments, were plastered everywhere. The floor was a mess, covered in clothes, and books were piled up on the chair and desk and even the foot of the bed. The bedclothes were twisted tightly. Surely no one could be sleeping here; this *couldn't* be a place of rest.

"Trout, I . . ."

Trout was frantically gathering things up. "I didn't want you to . . . I said *no*, didn't you hear me? Did Mum say you could . . . ?" He was practically sobbing.

"Trout, what is going on? What's happening to you?"

"I didn't want you to see. . . ."

"Trout, it's okay. Stop. Stop tidying. Look at me."

But he wouldn't. Undine gazed at the images on the walls. "What is this stuff?"

"It's just . . ." Trout stopped. "It's work. I'm working on something."

Undine looked at the notes. "Nothing is true," she read. "Everything is permitted." On another: "Mystery. Wildness. Immanence." And another: "Space Time Mass Energy Ether."

"It's the magic!" Undine realized. "Isn't it?"

Trout nodded.

"You're *studying* it?"

"Just in my spare time."

Undine's laugh was hollow and bitter. "Then you've got way too much spare time, Trout."

Trout sat on the bed. "I can't stop thinking about it."

"The magic?"

Trout hesitated. "Yes," he said. But there was something else, something he wasn't saying.

"What is it?"

"I . . ." his voice caught in his throat. "I can't. Please don't ask me."

"Is it . . . ?"

"I *can't*. Please."

Undine felt a hot surge of guilt burn through her. "Trout, I wish . . . I want . . ."

Trout closed his eyes, as if Undine was causing him physical pain.

"What are you doing here anyway?" Trout asked numbly.

Undine's news about Greece now seemed frivolous, empty. It wasn't even news; it was just a maybe. Once she had shared everything with Trout; now she couldn't say even the most ordinary things.

She opened her mouth and closed it again. "I just . . . I came to tell you something, that's all. It's not important."

"Is it about the magic?" Trout asked hungrily.

His intensity made her recoil. If she could have, she would have created a slit in space and crammed that word *magic* in it. It was amazing all the many covert ways it slithered into the jumble of normal words that made up the everyday, mundane conversations around her. Actually, she probably *could* have created that slit in space, but with the way the magic affected her, the whole world would have ended up crammed in it, turned inside out, like a beanbag stuffed through its own small zipper, the contents spilling away.

"No," Undine said. "It's nothing." She could feel the gap between them widening. It yawned cavernously—a space that she could physically have closed by just extending her arms, but a space that was so overwhelming she almost couldn't see her Trout at all, just this shallow copy of Trout, an echo.

Trout stared at the floor. Undine glanced around his room again. It was like being in the bedroom of a stranger. She looked at Trout. He sat, his face white and drawn. A memory of Trout's face revisited her: on the beach in her arms, his heart stopped, his body limp, his head lolling to one side so all she could see was one open, lifeless eye.

Undine couldn't be in that room for another moment.

In the hallway she forced herself to turn back and look at him.

"Trout?" she said.

"Yes."

"Do me a favor, okay?" She looked into his eyes and waited till his gaze met hers. "Please?"

Trout's eyes dropped away as if he knew what she was going to say. Already defeated, he nodded.

Undine glanced at the walls again and shivered. "Take it down, Trout. Take it all down."

Undine let herself out. The Montmorencys' door slammed shut. Outside she gulped a lungful of thin, cold air. The sky smelled faintly of woodsmoke and snow; it cleared her head. She ran up the steps, two at a time. Though she felt disloyal, with every step her heart felt lighter, and by the time she reached her own house she had entirely shed the burdensome presence of Trout.

CHAPTER FOUR

Trout woke as he always did, sitting up, gasping for breath, squeezing it out again. Breathing out was the difficulty, as if his body were trying to hoard air for some mysterious future purpose. It felt like drowning, only instead of water flooding his body, it was oxygen. Gradually the dream would subside; he would go from being his dream self, choked with darkness, to being his real, ordinary, living self again.

The dream was always the same.

Will darkness or light be born? Undine whispered, before putting her mouth to his, as he had so often longed for her to do. And then came the treachery:

she inhaled, stealing the air from his lungs.

His mother had thought that his asthma had returned and insisted he see his childhood doctor, Dr. Adams. The doctor's consulting rooms smelled of sickness and disinfectant. Trout was terrified of what his old, pale-faced doctor might see in him, looking that closely: studying his ear canals, shining light in his eyes, and listening to his breath.

"Say *ah*," the doctor said, probing in Trout's mouth with a tongue depressor.

"Aargh!" Trout wanted to scream.

When Dr. Adams put his stethoscope up against Trout's chest, Trout thought the doctor might hear nothing, just the swirl of silence. But the doctor had declared him healthy, and blamed stress for the attacks; his mother was easily convinced. Although it was only the beginning of winter, the teachers were already talking about final exams, assessment criteria, and university entrance scores.

Trout closed his eyes and focused on the imperative of breath. He made each exhalation slow and deliberate. He felt himself slipping back into the void of sleep and struggled awake. As soon as his eyes closed he could see Undine, hear her voice. *Baby*, she whispered. *Baby, here comes the dark*. He fought to keep his eyes open.

The illuminated clock by his bed said 12:14.

Hanging on a hook by the front door was an old winter coat that was used by all the males in the Montmorency family; Trout wore it on his nighttime excursions. One morning someone had commented on the coat's dampness. Trout worried it would lead them to him but, though curious, no Montmorency had considered the matter worthy of investigation. Anyway, from Trout's point of view, it was better to use the communal coat than draw his mother's astute attention to the extra wear and laundering of his own fleecy jacket.

Despite the weight of the woollen coat, outside the cold air shocked him, and he walked briskly as if to outpace it.

He always walked with purpose, though he rarely

had a destination in mind. Every night he took a different route, making his decision to turn left or right spontaneously. The decision was random. Sometimes if he felt himself inclined to go left, he would deliberately turn right, as if to ward off any subconscious pattern that might be forming.

Sometimes the direction he took was influenced by other factors, such as the presence of an individual or a couple. These he avoided: the intimacy of the street at night was too much for him. Groups he didn't mind so much. He felt threatened by them, yes, there was danger in the restlessness of youths when they collected en masse. But he liked the danger, it fed him somehow, lent him an energy he needed; gave him life, he supposed, where life was lacking.

Once he had walked halfway up the mountain. That night he had almost been hit by a car; it sped around a blind corner and skidded onto the wrong side of the road. It stopped just short of Trout, and the engine failed. Noise filled his ears in the moment the car approached, but its stillness was more crushing, more deafening. There were no houses nearby, just gum trees staggered down the steep embankment to his left. With the dazzling headlights in his eyes, Trout had not been able to make out the driver, or if there were any passengers. In that instant, though, they were all caught in the same story, watching the alternative outcome unfolding before them. Then the motor started and the car reversed away from Trout. The headlights swung away, and Trout was left with the shape of them burned temporarily on his retinas before he began the long journey homeward.

Tonight he found himself drawn to a group of three girls. They were older than him, but not much. At first he thought they were drunk; they screeched and whooped with laughter, talking over the top of one another, words crowding the sky around them like fluttering night birds. But they were walking too decisively; they had a mission, they had a destination.

There was one—she was attractive in a brittle, peevish kind of way—she was the leader. The others were larger than her, taller; one was quite fat. They were her minions: by their sheer bulk they would seem to dominate, but they would always do what she said. As the large feel about the small—as Trout felt about Undine—they would be compelled by blind, stupid instinct to protect her.

To say he decided to follow them would be overstating the case. Simply he found himself caught up in their wake; he trailed closely behind them. They did not appear to notice him but this, he knew, was his special talent, his superpower. He had always blended into the background of things.

One of the girls, he observed, was carrying a brick, or rather half a brick, her long fingers wrapped around it. Another had a plastic bag with a heavy tub in it; she shifted it from hand to hand as if the weight was burdensome. The small one carried nothing. She spoke more quietly than the others; her voice was high and thin and she had the hint of a captivating sibilant lisp. Her face was pale and flattish and heart shaped; her hair was dark with the faintest insinuation of curl. She was the one who caught his eye. She was *meant* to; she had carefully arranged it to be so. She was the type to surround herself with people who, neither ugly nor beautiful, would always fail to capture someone's interest.

Trout overtook the girls, knowing it was less conspicuous to seem to be in the lead than following behind. He passed them, walking slightly onto the road, conveying the vague impression that he had been trying to overtake for some time. The largest girl glanced at him perfunctorily; clearly she considered it her role to physically protect the group, but as Trout posed no threat, her eyes passed over him, glazed, barely registering him. The small one, the leader, didn't even look up. On closer inspection, Trout saw that her nose was slightly snubbed, her pale skin freckled. She clearly had the capacity to appear quite plain, ugly even. Beauty works in mysterious ways.

They traveled down one of the main roads that intersected the city, past the park, turning left into Battery Point. This was a suburb of tightly packed streets, as precise and as old as the interior mechanism of an antique watch. It was a suburb of old rich people and students: close walking distance to the university, the art school, and the conservatorium of music as well as the market, the wharf, and the city.

On the other side of the road, Trout matched their pace. As they progressed through the streets, past the sleeping houses, the girls grew quiet and purposeful. They arrived finally at a weatherboard house that had been converted into two flats, one upstairs, one down. The brick was placed aside for the moment; it was the plastic bag's contents that were of immediate interest. Trout stood in the shadows, largely concealed by parked cars, watching as the girls produced a tin of paint and three brushes. They set to work on different sections of the concrete driveway, the occasional giggle or exclamation erupting, quickly answered by violent shushing.

After a short period the larger girls put down their brushes. The small girl kept writing. The other two were clearly getting jumpy.

"Come on," they hissed, despite the fact that the downstairs flat remained dark and quiet, the occupants clearly unaware of what was going on outside.

"Come *on*."

The girl got up, admired her work, and dusted off her hands. They dropped the brushes and the tin back in the bag. There were some more fierce whispers among the girls before the large one picked up the brick and hurled it at the house. It missed the window and hit the front door with a loud crack that rang through the street. The girls ran. They dispersed, confused. Two ran away from Trout up the street, squealing and laughing, jumping into a garden to hide. The third—she was neither fat nor thin, but she was cumbersome and heavy-footed—ran straight past Trout. He could hear her breathing in short, ragged gasps. Her face was white and strained, with guilt perhaps, or with the fear of being caught. She stopped a little distance away and regretfully watched the other two girls disappearing into the garden. Then, her hand pressed against her side as if she had a stitch, she kept walking in the direction she had been running, alone.

Trout could not see what was written on the driveway. He stepped forward to read it, but before he had a chance to, a yellow light illuminated the front door and it opened. A tall, bony girl with white-blond hair looked straight at him. Her hair looked slept on; her feet were bare in the cold winter air. She wore a blue singlet and men's pajama bottoms. Her gaze seemed to slice through him, like a knife cutting into the soft underbelly of a fish.

She looked down at the driveway. She read one of the messages, tilting her head. She walked down and read all of them, her icy blue eyes widening with disbelief. She cupped her hands over her mouth and said something into them that Trout couldn't hear. He was rooted to the ground, cursed by his inaction as her eyes began to leak tears.

She walked up the driveway and looked left and right to the ends of the street.

"What does she want from me?" she said,

mystified—to Trout, to the street, to the winter air? Trout couldn't be sure. She hadn't looked at him, not directly, but surely she must be aware that he was there. "She can keep him. It's nothing to do with me now."

Trout had no answer. His heart hammered. His ribs ached. His voice was caged in his throat; he wanted to release it. But as he tried to choke sound out of his dry throat, she turned, still without looking at him, and went back to her flat. At the door she rubbed halfheartedly at the black mark the brick had left on the white paintwork. She stooped to pick up the brick and took it with her inside her flat.

When Trout walked back up the street toward home, the three girls had gone; there was no sign of them. The night that they had come from had swallowed them whole.

CHAPTER FIVE

There was a particular smell in the math classroom, like old rubber and stale air and past students, as if the heater had stored up the same smell from previous years and then released an older, more unpleasant version of it. Undine hated math first thing in the morning; her breakfast churned in her stomach as soon as the smell hit her.

"Are you and Dominic coming to Duncan's birthday party?"

Duncan was Fran's boyfriend. He was at uni, in his third year studying medicine, and was friends with Trout's brothers.

"When is it? I'll have to check with Lou."

"It's next month. Please come," Fran begged. "It's so much better when you're there."

"I'll try."

"Grunt will be there." Fran poked her, grinning wickedly.

Undine poked Fran back. "So? I have a boyfriend, remember?"

But Undine felt the hairs on her head prickle at the roots at the thought of seeing Grunt—Alastair—again. She hadn't seen him alone since the Bay of Angels the year before, though sometimes she went to a uni party with Fran and he would be there: gentle, attentive, remote, unattainable.

Trout came in late. He hadn't been on the bus again. Undine observed him from where she sat with Fran at the back of the room. He was tired, gray, and kind of washed out, as if a small internal tide was grinding him down.

"He looks terrible," Fran murmured.

"Trevor Montmorency," intoned Mr. Anderson.

"Late again? We are going through the homework from last Friday. I trust you've done it."

Trout mumbled an excuse as he sat down. Mr. Anderson leaned over him and spoke in a muted, impatient tone. Undine knew the speech; the teachers all used some version of it: "letting yourself down . . . final exams . . . the most important year of your life . . . expected better from you . . . sorely disappointed . . ."

"My father has invited me to go to Greece with him," Undine told Fran. She didn't want to talk about Trout; she felt weighed down by the responsibility of him, the changes he had clearly undergone since last summer. She did not understand exactly what had changed him, and in fact the change had come so gradually that it was impossible to name the point where regular Trout had slipped away.

"Really?" Fran squealed. Mr. Anderson glared at her. "I am so madly jealous! When?"

"I'd be away for the September break, and then the first two weeks of next term, so four weeks holiday."

"That's less than six weeks away! Oh, heaven," sighed Fran enviously. "Greece."

"Lou hasn't exactly said yes yet. But she hasn't said no."

"She'll say yes. She has to. It's Greece!"

Undine snorted. She wasn't sure if Fran's logic would work on Lou.

Trout and Undine sat together on the bus, not speaking. Glimpses of the river, as smooth and gray as a sheet of metal dividing the land, flashed between the trees, telegraph poles, and houses on their right. Already Undine could taste the dark coming. Night fell early in winter. It would not be long before the sun set, long streams of rosy pink or bright orange streaking out from behind the hazy blue mountain.

Trout shrank away from the window, leaning toward the aisle of the bus.

"Are you okay?" Undine asked.

He looked at her sideways, as though he hadn't

even the energy, or perhaps the will, to turn his head.

"I wish you would stop asking me that," he said wearily. "I'm fine."

Undine sighed and looked out the window again. She glanced back. Trout's head was down; he stared at a point in space between him and the floor. He seemed so . . . *sad* wasn't quite the right word. Depleted. Kind of finished. She was frightened for him.

She reached out and touched his hand. Trout's face softened. His fingers took hers, and held them.

It was surprising to Undine, how alien his skin felt against hers. As friends they rarely touched. She was suddenly embarrassed by it, the touching. She wanted to withdraw her hand—it twitched involuntarily—but she didn't want to hurt Trout's feelings. The bus stopped; his hand slipped from hers. They didn't make eye contact. But Trout seemed to sink even deeper inside himself. They disembarked from the bus and, wordlessly, they parted.

● ● ●

That night, breaking his own promise to himself to be random, Trout found himself walking through Fitzroy Gardens—the empty swings swaying slightly in the breeze as if remembering children past—and over Sandy Bay Road back to Battery Point. The writing on the driveway had gone, scrubbed away; all evidence of the event he had witnessed had vanished. The night was like that, transient, temporary. It left its scars, but not where anyone could see them.

He'd seen what he came to see. "So walk away," he said out loud. But he found himself creeping down the length of the driveway ninja style—toes first— to where the concrete broke up into rubble and the lawn messily began. At the back of the house the windows went from ceiling to floor, though curtains were drawn all around to keep out the cold night, to keep out the eyes of strangers who might plant themselves in the garden as Trout had done.

Visible through the curtains was a thin crack of light, and Trout found he was inexorably drawn to it, his heart fluttering like a moth at an exposed bulb.

She was awake, reading by lamplight. Trout edged closer. She sat sideways in the chair, at first Trout thought in a picture of peaceful repose. But he realized she often glanced up at the front door, twitching nervously when a dog barked or a car drove past or when the wind played the walnut tree like an old creaking cello. (Trout jumped with her at every sound.)

She turned the page of her book back and forth. Trout recognized her insomnia. She was afraid to go to sleep, in case those girls returned.

It struck Trout that somehow their individual lives had become concurrent; they were bound together by their separate roles—victim, witness—in the same small drama. She rose; she moved toward the crack in the curtains where he was standing. She shivered. Suddenly, for the briefest of moments, he wanted her to see him. He wanted to be seen, to be observed, to have his existence confirmed; suddenly he was afraid if no one looked directly at him, he might disappear altogether.

48

She flicked the curtain fully closed.

He ninja-walked back to the road; as soon as his feet touched the footpath he broke into a run. He pounded his feet heavily on the concrete, but his shoes were soft-soled and the terraced rows of sandstone houses on either side of the street seemed to absorb the noise, so despite his carelessness he made little noise, little impact on the sleeping city.

When he got home, he let himself in with care. He slipped out of the coat and nudged off his shoes.

From the bottom of the stairs, he saw the blue flickering light of the television emanating from the lounge room. He felt a jolt of alarm—was someone waiting up for him? He walked softly toward the room and peered in.

His father was sitting in one of the soft creaky armchairs, watching an infomercial with an expression of incredulity on his face. He noticed Trout.

"Oh," he said. "Did I wake you? I couldn't sleep."

"Me neither," said Trout. His father didn't ask him why he was dressed, or even seem to notice.

"I'm not sure what this thing is," said Mr. Montmorency. "But I feel a strange urge to buy it."

Trout settled down into the other armchair. He found the garish colors and the plastic, buoyant tone of the presenters soothing, and here, sitting next to his dad, he allowed himself to close his eyes for a minute and sleep.

CHAPTER SIX

The weekend did not look encouraging. The clouds were gray and low, bearing down heavily on the earth. Lou was doing the laundry, and the smell of washing powder and lavender oil filled the house oppressively. Even the dryer had a particular smell, of hot crisp air and baked clothes. The heater was on, the house was warm, but somehow the cold seemed to penetrate Undine's mood, and she walked about the house restlessly, unable to settle on anything.

Lou observed Undine's mood for a while—Jasper too was bored and fidgety, tipping toys recklessly out on the floor only to abandon them—then said casually, "I rang the publisher yesterday." Lou worked as a freelance book indexer, mainly for one particular publisher on the mainland. "They are happy to shift my workload around a bit so I can take the time off."

"So that means . . . ?" Undine gasped excitedly.

"There are conditions."

"Yes. Yes. I'll take schoolwork with me. I'll pass my exams with flying colors, whatever that means."

Lou was stern. "No magic. Not you. Not Prospero."

"Oh, Lou, I promise. Thank you, *thank you*." Undine threw her arms around Lou.

"Undine, I mean it. No matter what he says. He can be very persuasive."

"Lou, honestly, I don't even *want* to use the magic. After what happened last year, when Trout nearly . . . I nearly lost everyone. Prospero understands why I want to wait." Undine hesitated. She thought of the pictures she had seen of Greece, white rocky islands surrounded by impossibly blue sea. The magic—*her* magic—was tied to the sea somehow, or at least to the bay where Prospero had lived. She remembered what it had been like the first time she'd seen the sea, how the noise of it had filled her. She wondered if she would be strong enough to keep her promise to Lou when surrounded by all that blue.

"Lou," Undine said, gently but firmly, and she was addressing herself as well, "I have already made a promise to you—no magic till I finish school, and then we'll explore it together. We promised each other. And I meant it—here or in Greece—no magic."

Lou raised an eyebrow; was she unconvinced? But she went on. "It occurs to me that we should ask someone to look after the house. Perhaps one of the Montmorency boys?"

Undine could see that Lou didn't want Undine to over-enthuse. Excitement simmered inside her, but she kept it in check. Until they were actually on the plane, it wouldn't do to annoy Lou in any way.

"Trout?" she asked. It would be a fantastic gift for him. He'd love it, a house to himself for four weeks. It might, Undine dared to think, fix things between them, just a little.

Lou frowned. "I was thinking the oldest one. You know, what's his name? The one you . . ."

"Don't say it," moaned Undine. "You *can't* ask him."

Undine was still embarrassed when she thought of Trout's oldest brother, Richard, who she'd kissed, and more . . . almost a lot more. It hadn't really meant anything—to her or to Richard, but it had to Trout. He had seen them kissing, and she knew it was still painful for him to think about Undine and Richard together.

"Please. Not Richard. Can't we ask Trout?"

"All right. I was only half serious. Do you think Trout's mother would let him? She keeps those boys tied pretty close to her apron strings, doesn't she?"

"But we can ask? You could talk to her. . . ."

"See if he wants to come for brunch. We can ask Trout first, together. If he's keen, I'll talk to his mum."

Lazily, Undine climbed up to her room and looked from her window into Trout's. They had often communicated like this in the past, through arm waving and a complex language of signaling they had devised when still in primary school.

He was there, sitting right by the window. She waved at him to get his attention, but he didn't look up. Well. Signals were only good if whoever you were signaling was watching. She opened the French window and stepped out onto the balcony. The day was damp and cold; it seeped into her skin as soon as it made contact.

"Hey!" Undine yelled unceremoniously. "Trout!"

He looked up. She waved to him, beckoning him. "Pancakes!" she shouted. He looked kind of annoyed, but who can pass up pancakes? He hesitated, then nodded brusquely.

Trout climbed the concrete steps slowly, his sleep-deprived body aching. Each step seemed an immense effort, his own body too burdensome a weight to heave upward. Gravity fought him. Gravity sucks, thought Trout, and smiled despite himself at his inadvertent pun.

Undine met him at the front door. He wanted to share his stupid joke with her, but she was running on nervous energy, jumpy and too eager, and it made him clam up. Lou and Jasper were making pancakes in the kitchen.

"Hello, Trout," said Lou warmly. She had seemed to grow fonder of Trout since the summer, but he responded warily to this fondness. Trout still believed there was something fundamentally duplicitous and deceitful about Lou's behavior, concealing the magic from Undine for all those years. Lou had lied about Prospero, saying he was dead when he was alive (although, Trout thought now, perhaps that was only half a lie, for Prospero seemed to live only half a life). And since the summer, Lou had made Undine agree to leave the magic to rest until she finished school; she had refused to answer any questions about it, saying there was plenty of time for questions after Undine had finished her exams.

"But aren't you dying to know?" Trout asked Undine. He certainly was: his need to know more about the magic twisted inside him, winding around his guts, like cotton thread around the tip of a finger, cutting off the circulation.

"I can't make her tell me," Undine had said.

You could, thought Trout. If you really wanted to. You could fight. You could rage and scream. You could threaten. You could . . .

But, "I don't want to," Undine had answered his unspoken thoughts. "I hated it last year, when Lou and I were fighting. I just want us to be a family. Sometimes I think if I could pack the magic up, put it in a box, bury it deep underground . . . What if I don't want to know? It could change things. . . ." She'd shuddered. "She'll tell me. When she's ready. When I'm ready."

Trout frowned at the memory.

"Is there anything I can do?" he asked Lou politely. Jasper was still stirring the batter seriously, although half the pancakes had been made.

"Not really. Except you can keep that one occupied till I serve up." She pointed with her spatula at Undine, who was running her finger round the rim of the syrup jug, stealing a taste.

The sweet smell of pancakes and syrup, mingling with the hot fragrance of freshly washed clothes, made Trout heavy-lidded. He and Undine sat together on the couch.

"Are you going to Duncan's party?" she asked Trout.

Trout remembered Duncan's party with effort. "I don't know. Are you?"

"I told Fran I would."

Trout nodded. Undine picked at a thread on the couch. They were both relieved when Lou brought the pancakes out.

"Did Undine tell you?" Lou asked when they were all sitting at the table. "We've got a favor to ask."

Undine beamed into Trout's face.

Trout looked from Undine to Lou.

"Undine's told you about Greece."

"Um . . ."

"That Prospero has invited all of us to go with him?"

For a wild, irrational moment Trout thought they were going to ask him to go with them.

"Well, we were wondering, with your parents' permission of course, if you would house-sit while we're away. About four weeks. It would give you a quiet place to study, and you can make sure the house doesn't fall down in our absence."

Trout turned it over in his mind.

"That sounds good," he said slowly; then, warming to the idea, he admitted, "It sounds *great*."

"Well," said Lou. "Good. That works out for all of us. I'll ring your mother this afternoon."

After brunch, Trout and Undine sat on the couch again. Jasper busied himself on the floor in front of them. A cartoon played on the television. An ad came on, shouting at them to buy this, or do that, and Trout realized he had no memory of what they had been watching.

"Do you think your mum will let you?" Undine asked Trout.

"What? Oh, house-sit. Yeah. I think so."

They sank back into silence but, Trout perceived, it was an easier one; the television and the thought of Undine and Lou's proffered favor filled it nicely.

Jasper, as if he'd just remembered something, turned abruptly and examined Trout. His gaze was penetrating and Trout found it disconcerting; the temporary ease he had been feeling evaporated.

"Where do you go?" Jasper asked him.

Trout was not overly comfortable with Jasper. He did not have an easy rapport with small children; they made him feel enormous and oafish and strangely shy.

"What?"

"At nighttime. In the middle of the night. I seen you. Where do you go?"

"I . . ." Trout was at a loss.

"Jasper, you're making it up," Undine said.

"No, I'm not. I open my eyes like this in the middle of the night. My eyes are big, bigger, biggest. And I creep, creep to the window and I look. I creep like this," and he showed them.

"Well, that's very naughty," teased Undine delightedly. "Creep, creeping around in the middle of the night." To Trout she said, "He's just playing, telling a story."

It didn't seem like Jasper was playing, like he was making up stories. He couldn't have really seen Trout, could he? But Trout felt his face grow hot. He felt sick at the idea that he was being observed, even by Jasper.

"Where *do* you go in the middle of the night?" Undine said, but now she was teasing him. He tried to think of a glib answer, something offbeat and casual, but it wouldn't come.

"It's not a story." Jasper was nearly crying. "I *seen* you."

Trout looked at Undine and shook his head helplessly.

"It's all right, Jasper," she said. She didn't seem to notice Trout's discomfort. "We believe you. Don't we?"

Jasper looked at Trout and half shut his eyes. When he opened them again he said, "When I swing, I swing really high, and I kick the tree and it turns into a lovely sea horse and I kick the tree and it turns into a beautiful house. I swing high, higher, highest and I kick like this. I can kick you."

Undine said, "No, Jasper, that's not very nice. We don't kick our friends."

When Undine went to the kitchen to get drinks, Jasper turned to Trout again. "I seen you," he said bitterly. His face was transformed by his anger, narrow and wolfish; his whole body quivered. "One day I will be big, bigger, biggest. Bigger 'n you, and I will follow you."

Trout stared at him: he stared at him until Jasper dropped his gaze and looked away. And though it was cheap, Trout experienced a moment of pleasure that he had beaten Jasper with his stare.

"He's just a little kid," Trout told himself.

But that night Trout felt that Undine's house had eyes, that it watched him navigate his way through the dark.

In the city he walked past a group of young men. They were carrying half a case of beer; the rest seemed to be sloshing around in their bellies. Trout tensed. But as had happened at the girl's flat the night before, he found he wanted them to see him. He wanted something to happen to him; he wanted an outside force to act upon him.

As he approached, one of them threw an empty bottle into a car park. The bottle shattered and the men jeered. Time hovered for Trout; he stood poised against the next second, blood coursing through him. He met the gaze of one of the men. The stranger's eyes narrowed. Trout held his breath. And then the moment was over. The men passed him, and Trout dissolved into the cool night air. He was gone.

CHAPTER SEVEN

Undine watched the progression of dates on the calendar with growing excitement. Prospero sent tickets for all of them; he had insisted on paying Lou's and Jasper's fares in addition to Undine's. The tickets sat on the mantelpiece in the living room, and every time Undine saw them a warm flicker of anticipation danced in her belly.

The weekend before they were due to leave was Duncan's party. Undine and Trout were both going, but Dominic was not; it was his mother's birthday, and his family took birthdays very seriously.

"I can't believe I can't come," he murmured

earnestly at Undine. But, guiltily, she didn't mind him not coming. She found having a boyfriend tiring; the constant attention wore her down, and she felt eroded by his eyes, his fawning hands, by his romantic gestures. Perhaps it was the pull of the magic, or perhaps, as Lou suggested, the boys had simply grown into her. Whatever the case, when Undine had started the school year, suddenly she had admirers. Overwhelmed, she had chosen Dominic and stuck with him. He was attractive in a smooth, shiny way; she knew he was considered a catch. Girls gave her looks in the hallway—envious or bitter— and she felt a little sorry that he was wasted on her when there were clearly other girls who would appreciate him more.

"Oh, well," said Undine. "It's only one party. There'll be others." But of course it was the wrong thing to say—this party was different because she would soon be away for four whole weeks and they would miss each other so much. Dominic sulked until Undine grew annoyed with him. She sighed with relief when

she hung up the phone: their good-byes had been suf-
ficiently earnest to placate Dominic.

She found she was looking forward to the party. A
chance to relax, to let her hair down, to dance, to play.

"It's not too late to cancel the trip," Lou warned
on the night of the party, following her up the stairs
to her bedroom.

"I know, I know."

"I mean it. Give me one reason and *pfft*"—Lou
clicked her fingers—"no more Greece. So no funny
business, okay?"

Undine took Lou by the shoulders. "Who are you
and what have you done to my mother?"

"Ha-ha."

"Seriously, Lou, when did you turn into this
person? Although my eighteenth birthday is a few
measly months away, I will not be drinking. Nor will
I be doing hard drugs, stripping in a sleazy dive, or
having Bob Dylan's love child."

Lou screwed up her face. "Bob Dylan? Ew. He's,
like, all old and stuff."

"Stop trying to speak like the young people," Undine scolded.

"Okay, but I do mean it."

"What, that Bob Dylan's old?"

"Well, yeah. But also, I want you to make sensible choices tonight." Lou sat on Undine's bed and Undine sat next to her.

"Oh, god, Lou, do you mean sex?"

"Among other things."

"Do we have to talk about this? Dominic isn't even going to be there."

"I sort of think we should. I mean, we haven't talked much about this stuff before. Not since you've been . . . older."

"I know how babies are made, if that's what you mean."

"I'd rather you know how babies are *not* made! But it's more than that. Sex—"

"We haven't *had* sex!"

"I believe you. I just want to say that sex *is* a big deal. Sometimes it probably doesn't feel like it, with magazines and television and your friends and ads for soft drinks telling you to just do it. But there *are* right reasons and wrong reasons for doing it."

"I know."

"Do you? I don't know, when I was your age . . . it felt like such a burden. Virginity, I mean. Something to offload as soon as possible."

Undine said nothing, but she could relate to that feeling.

"And then," Lou went on, "once you went so far, it felt like there was no going back, no putting it away for later. Do you know what I mean?" Suddenly Undine wondered if Lou was just talking about sex or whether this was a roundabout way of talking about the magic, too.

"I guess so."

"Look, I'm not saying it will ruin your life if you don't wait. Or that you have to wait till you're married. But, well, wait at least till you really like the person. Till you're over that first heady, exhilarating rush and you're really comfortable with them. The longer you wait, believe me, the better it is."

"Is that all? This conversation is totally embarrassing."

Lou threw her hands up. "Okay, okay. Mothers have to have sex, you know, or they wouldn't be mothers."

"Stop saying the word *sex*!"

Lou laughed. "Get ready. You're a gorgeous girl, you know that?"

"You have to say that, 'cause you're my mum."

"Nope. I just tells it like I sees it."

"You're not wearing those?" said Mrs. M. as Trout came down in the black jeans and long-sleeved T-shirt he wore every day. "It's a party," she cajoled. "It's festive. Wear something . . ."

"Festive?" Trout supplied dryly.

"What about a shirt? Something more cheerful. Something *colorful*."

Trout rolled his eyes. "Mum," he said. "You don't know anything! No one is going to be wearing a shirt. . . ."

Dan came downstairs in a shirt: clinging purple polyester.

"There," said Mrs. M. "Doesn't Dan look smart?"

"*Smart?*" exclaimed Dan, and he started undoing the buttons on his shirt, revealing a black raglan T-shirt underneath. "Right, that's it. I'm changing. I don't know why I let you talk me into it in the first place. Taking fashion advice from my mother! What would the guys think?"

"You're such nice-looking, well-brought-up boys," lamented Mrs. M. "Why do you have to hide in all that black? Why do you have to go out looking so *drab*?"

Trout looked at Dan. "*Because* we're nice-looking, well-brought-up boys."

Mrs. M. shook her head and returned to the kitchen muttering. "I would have thought . . . the right girl . . . surely a good, well-mannered boy . . . even in this day and age . . ."

Dan eased himself back into the purple shirt and winked at Trout. "Are you really wearing that?" Dan looked at Trout's black attire appraisingly. "You can borrow something of mine."

"Shhh," said Trout. "Not too loud or Mum'll wet herself with excitement. She'll think we've finally turned into the daughters she always wanted." But he followed Dan up to his room and sat on the bed while Dan rifled through his drawers.

"Here," said Dan, and passed Trout a coarse green poplin shirt with a pointy collar. "It used to be Dad's, back when he was young. And thin. And not a complete spaz. It'll look good on you, with your girly complexion and fair hair."

"Thanks a lot."

But the shirt fitted well, and Trout felt himself faintly changed by it. He observed himself in the mirror on Dan's wardrobe door. The shirt made him look older, and, because of its striking, almost ugly character, surer of himself. The color did set off his fair skin and made his eyes appear a true blue, instead of the murky gray they tended toward normally. It hung well on his shoulders, and his slight frame seemed like an asset instead of an accident of birth.

"Hmm," Dan considered, tilting his head. "Yep, it suits you. You can have that if you want."

"Thanks! Oh, by the way . . ." Trout thought he should take advantage of this new, generous Dan. "Can we give Undine a lift to the party?"

In response, Dan grunted.

"Is that a yes?"

Dan shrugged. "I suppose."

"You don't like her much, do you?"

"Not really."

Half of Trout was pained to hear it; the other half took a curious pleasure in Dan's dislike of her. It was a baffling business, unrequited love. He wondered if he should defend her, but found he didn't particularly *want* to.

Confused, Trout simply said, "I'll meet you at the car," and headed out to pick up Undine. Outside the night was crisp and clear and still. He felt a jump of anticipation in his stomach. He was looking forward to the party. He was looking forward to being out with Undine, without Dominic clinging to her like a soft, naked mollusk. Dominic was all right; he was pleasant enough, one of those boys who'd become popular by being an all-round Mr. Nice Guy. But as much as Trout suspected Undine's ambivalence toward her boyfriend, it wasn't easy to see someone else have a claim on her, physically at least, if not on her heart.

"Wow," said Undine as she answered the door to Trout. "You look . . . so different."

"Different good or different bad?"

Lou came up behind Undine. "Trout! You look amazing." She gave Undine a little push. "See, I told you to wear a dress."

Undine rolled her eyes. But as soon as Lou was out of earshot, she whispered self-consciously to Trout, "Do you think I should change?"

"It's just a party," he said. "You look great."

She did look great, in faded bootleg jeans and a soft, coal-black, V-neck jumper that tied with a belt around the waist. Her hair was pinned close to her head, and she was wearing a lipstick that looked like liquid gold and a tiny amount of black pencil under her eyes. It was low-key, but she looked . . . *stunning*, he thought jadedly.

Dan was warming the car. Trout offered Undine the front passenger seat but, glancing at Dan's hard-set jaw, she declined and slipped into the back. They drove up the Southern Outlet and turned left onto the road that swung up Mount Nelson, a hilly suburb that had retained large tracts of bush. Duncan's house was near the top, on a large block of land abutting the old signal station.

When Undine and Trout arrived, Dan having dissolved even before they reached the front gate, the party swept them up straightaway. What seemed like a hundred people were scattered through the bush. Duncan had set up an outdoor dance floor; techno pumped through the bush. A huge wire bird strung with fairy lights teetered perilously, overlooking the dancers.

"Let's dance," Undine shouted over the music.

"I don't *do* dancing," protested Trout, but he found that in the green shirt he did. He and Undine danced, together but not touching. He forced himself to stop counting the beat. He shut his eyes and just moved, letting the music propel his feet and arms. The music was hard and fast; he could feel the vibrations in his breastplate, resonating through the core of him.

He moved away from Undine, finding a private space, and danced. It was cathartic, it was liberating. The green shirt released him, it transformed him. Under the wire bird, he felt part bird himself. He whirled, he soared.

CHAPTER EIGHT

Undine left Trout dancing alone, his face radiant. She drifted around the edge of the party, trying not to scan the clusters of people for Grunt. But when she did catch sight of him, leaning against a tree talking to Dan and others she didn't know, her heart flickered. His eyes found hers and he smiled, slow and easy. But he did not leave the group he was with, and Undine felt too shy to join him.

She found herself at Duncan's fence line, looking through the bush to the flat park area of the old signal station. From the lookout you had a view of the city and Tasman Bridge in one direction; then your gaze swept over the Eastern Shore and down the D'Entrecasteaux Channel past the Iron Pot to Storm Bay and the northern tip of Bruny Island. Stephen used to bring her up here to watch fireworks over the Derwent on New Year's Eve. She felt the familiar but acute twist in her gut of missing Stephen. It came on her like this, the grief: sudden, usually fleeting, but always painful. Now it took her breath from her.

Prospero was her biological father, and from the moment she had seen him she had *recognized* him somehow. A part of her that had been longing for a father was almost satisfied by Prospero. But the shape of that longing and the shape of Prospero didn't always match; there were gaps where the longing slipped through. Undine knew this was because deep down she would always be Stephen's daughter, too, that she would truly belong also to him.

With her mind, she reached out, searching for Stephen. Sometimes it was like he was just out of reach, as if she could almost . . . if only . . . Since the magic, since the world had opened like a flower, revealing hidden, secret parts, Undine had begun to think more about Stephen; about death. What had seemed so final before, so constant, now felt . . . negotiable. Like there might be a way to undo what had been done.

Was death more powerful than magic? Could she— she dared to think it—could she bring Stephen back? The stars winked enigmatically and refused to answer.

The magic was so unstable. She dared not use it to light so much as a candle flame. How could she ever channel it to perform something so specific, so delicate; how could she ask it to light something so infinitely complex as a human being?

Something crashed through the trees behind her.

"There you are!" It was Duncan and Fran, their legs tied together as if they were in a three-legged race. Fran's face shone.

"Are you drunk?" Undine teased, laughing at their sudden appearance, relieved to be distracted from her thoughts.

"Are we drunk?" Fran asked Duncan.

Duncan considered the question. "*You* might be drunk. I am merely high on life."

"Come on, you pair of lushes." Undine helped manhandle them to face the other direction, and they returned to the party together.

Trout came off the dance floor thirsty. He looked around for water, but found only beer. He opened it and at first sipped tentatively, but his thirst raged and soon it was gone.

"Great shirt," a girl said.

He squinted at her; it was hard to see in the dark. "Thanks."

"Aren't you Trevor Montmorency?" She was wearing a tie-dyed dress that billowed around her. Her hair was knotted up with feathers and what looked like a dried chicken bone.

"Trout," he corrected her, though he was surprised

that she recognized him. Perhaps she was a friend of one of his brothers.

"That's right, Trout," the girl repeated with a slow smile, as if she were tasting his name. "Trout. Wanna have an adventure, Trout?"

"No," said Trout. "Thanks all the same." Or at least that's what he intended to say. But the green shirt spoke for him. "Yes."

Before he really knew what was happening, the girl had stuck out her finger. On it was a strangely small piece of paper.

"Put it under your tongue," she said.

Inside the green shirt, Trout was, after all, still Trout. He hesitated.

"It's all right," she said. "It's only a taste; it won't hurt you. It'll just make the colors look pretty and you'll go like Cathy Freeman all night."

Trout touched the tip of her finger with his tongue, and tasted both the saltiness of human finger and the metallic chemicals on the paper.

"Here," the girl said, handing him another beer. "Wash it down with this."

Trout threw his head back and drank.

Undine found Trout dancing. He was still beaming, but his dancing had taken on a frantic yet oddly introspective quality.

"Undine!" he said when he saw her. He came over, breathless, and put his arm round her shoulder, sagging so she bore some of his weight. "What are you doing? Do you want a beer?"

"No, thanks."

Trout was unselfconsciously rubbing her arm. Undine's black jumper was thin and ineffective against the wintry air, and Trout's body felt warm against hers. Undine found herself leaning into him. She shivered.

"You cold?" he asked.

She nodded. He tightened his arm around her. He wasn't looking at her, but watching the dancers twisting and bowing under the trees.

"Warming up?"

Undine could feel his voice vibrating through his chest. She was confused. It felt a comfortable, safe place to be, and yet tonight Trout seemed like a stranger, more confident, not just in his manner but in his body, the way he embraced her when usually he jumped a mile if their hands brushed.

"Trout, I—"

He looked down and their eyes met. There was such intensity in his gaze that her breath caught in her throat. Fleetingly, she thought he was going to kiss her. Fleetingly, she thought she *wanted* him to.

Then from the throng of dancers a girl disengaged. "Trout!" she said, standing on the edge of the floor beckoning. "Are you dancing?"

"Dance?" Trout said, and he disappeared among them.

Undine was left reeling: relieved, disappointed.

• • •

The night whirled. The night spun. For Trout it occurred in flashes. *Flash*: he was dancing with the chicken-bone girl. *Flash*: Undine was with him, he was holding her, and she seemed like she wanted him to kiss her. *Flash*: Undine was gone and he was dancing, dancing. *Flash*: he was drinking another beer, he was laughing, he was kissing the chicken-bone girl. *Flash*: the chicken-bone girl had gone. Dan was there. He was saying, "Take it easy, little brother." *Flash*: he thought he saw the white-haired girl from the other night and he followed her, like Alice following the white rabbit. But he couldn't see her, and he couldn't remember why he was looking for her in the first place.

Flash. Trout was on his own, under the wire bird, and his heart pounded in his chest. Thoughts jumbled up in his mind; he could barely hold them together. The trees seemed to merge into each other, undulating from the roots up. What was real? He couldn't tell anymore. He looked at his own hand. It appeared different in the moonlight; he could make out individual scales on his skin, pale and silvery. Like a fish. Was he an impostor? What if the actual Trout had died on the beach? What if he was the fish, the changeling? And any minute the magic could drain out of him and here he was, so far from the sea. Was he the fish? Was he dead? Was Trout dead?

Will darkness or light be born?

And Trout found himself gasping for air. His knees buckled.

He couldn't breathe. He couldn't *breathe*.

Baby, here comes the dark.

CHAPTER NINE

Undine *warmed herself* by the small campfire Duncan had built. She looked up, noticing a small crowd forming at the dance area. She realized the music, which had been pumping a constant reverberating beat through the trees, had stopped.

Fran emerged from the crowd. "Undine," she called. "It's Trout."

Duncan was already at Trout's side when Undine pushed her way through the crowd. He'd wrapped Trout in his jacket; the green shirt was hidden within the brown folds. Trout was limp and white and barely conscious; his head kept lolling away from the water bottle Duncan was offering him. His breathing was labored, he wheezed and coughed. Undine stared aghast.

"It's all right," said Duncan. "I don't think he's in any danger. What's he taken?" Duncan asked the chicken-bone girl, who was hovering agitatedly at the periphery of the crowd.

"It was just a taste," she blubbed. "Honestly . . ."

Duncan snapped, "You gave him drugs? He's still in high school!"

"He said he wanted an adventure."

Duncan touched his forehead. "Some adventure. We need to keep him calm," he said to Undine. "And conscious. I'll go up to the house and run a bath. Undine, talk to him. If we can't get him calmed down, then we might have to call an ambulance." He looked at the chicken-bone girl. "And you. Piss off! I said, no drugs. I told you."

Undine talked gently in Trout's ear, stringing reassuring phrases together. He stopped wheezing, his breathing slowed, and though it was still faster and more shallow than usual, he didn't seem to be having any real difficulty.

But though his panic was subsiding, still he said, "I can't breathe. I can't . . ."

"You are breathing," Undine reassured him. "You're fine."

"You've got to turn me back. You've got to make it right."

"Trout, I don't understand. . . ."

"I'm not supposed to be here."

"Of course you are. You're at Duncan's party. You were invited. We all want you here."

"No, no," said Trout urgently. He tried to sit up. "I'm supposed to be dead. Or . . ."

"Trout! No."

Trout stopped, remembering. "Or not. Was it . . . a fish?"

Undine kept stroking his hair. "It was a fish, Trout. It was just a fish."

"I thought . . ." Trout seemed to be returning to himself. "I thought it was me. . . ."

Duncan came back with Grunt and Dan. They helped Trout up. Undine stood to follow them.

"You," said Dan viciously. "I don't *like* you."

Undine stopped, stung.

"This isn't the time," barked Duncan. "She's coming with us."

Undine waited in the lounge room while the boys took Trout into the bathroom. Fran made coffee in the kitchen. Undine sat forward, her insides tightly knotted, until finally she heard some splashing and the welcome sound of laughter from the bathroom. She slumped back, relieved.

So she was taken unawares when Dan came out and wheeled on her. "This is your fault," he accused.

"My fault? I didn't do anything." Her voice wavered; she struggled to keep herself steady.

"Yeah, right," Dan spat.

"What did I do?"

"Let's start with Richard. You *did* him. When you *knew* how Trout felt about you."

"I didn't *do* Richard! And how Trout feels about me is nothing I've done. I can't help it."

"Can't you? Did you ever, did you *ever* turn to Trout and say, there is no hope. Did you ever tell him that you didn't want him? Or did you keep him hanging, keep him interested, just in case?"

Undine felt the magic whip and burn inside her and she longed to unleash it, just for a moment, to strike out at Dan.

"He's my friend," Undine said. "He's my best friend. I didn't want to . . ."

"Your best friend! Do you treat all your friends that way? Besides, the point is, he doesn't want to be your *friend*, so it's not really the great friendship you think it is, is it? How can it ever be equal, when he loves you, and you just . . . You use him, and you used Richard, too." Dan shook his head in disgust. "You're some kind of evil. And now my man Grunt . . ."

"That's enough, Dan," Grunt said quietly, appearing in the doorway.

But Undine deflated. Dan was right. She had never outright rejected Trout. She'd always deflected, avoiding the topic. She'd been so busy trying to protect the friendship for her own selfish reasons that she hadn't been fair to Trout. She owed it to Trout to be honest with him.

"Just stay away from me," said Dan. "Stay away from all of us, or I'll . . ."

Grunt shook his head and almost smiled. "Believe me, you don't want to take *her* on."

Undine sucked her breath in. She wasn't sure if Grunt had meant his remark to sting, but it did. She turned, desperate to escape, but Dan wasn't finished with her. He jabbed his finger savagely, contradicting his last statement. "No, you should go to him," he said. "You go to my brother and you tell him—"

"Tell me what?"

Trout stood at the doorway. He was trembling, his skin still pallid and wan, but he looked much improved.

"Trout! Are you okay?"

He asked again, "Tell me what?"

Dan crossed his arms and nodded at Undine. "Go on."

"Not now," Undine begged. "It's not the right time."

"The *right time* was years ago," Dan sneered. "Or at least last year, before you messed around with Richard."

Trout looked at Undine and then at Dan. In that moment it was clear by Trout's face that he'd worked out what Dan was asking of Undine."

"No," Trout begged. "No. I don't want to hear it."

"Trout," said Undine. "He's right. I should . . ."

Trout was desperate. "No. Don't. It won't make it better. It will make it worse. Please don't say it."

"Say it," Dan insisted to Undine.

"Shut up," Trout implored him. "Shut up."

Undine looked distraughtly from Trout to Dan.

"It's not like there's *no* hope," Trout said wildly,

addressing everyone in the room. "Things might change. She might . . ." He looked at Undine. "You *might*." He lowered his voice, murmuring to Undine, "What about tonight . . . I *remember*. We almost . . . didn't we?"

Undine stared at Trout, paralyzed. Could she really say there was no hope? In all the many possible futures that flowered before them, could she really say never ever? She hesitated. Their eyes met.

She shook her head. "Trout, no. I'm sorry. But my feelings will never change."

Trout crumpled. "I hate you!" he shouted at Dan. "What did you have to do that for?"

"I did it for you. You had to hear it."

"No," he said, and he meant it. "I didn't." His jaw was set, and his hands were clenched into fists. For an awful moment, Undine thought that Dan and Trout were actually going to fight, until Fran came in and broke the spell.

"Anyone for coffee?" she asked, with a cup in her

hand. "You should have one, Trout. You look bloody awful."

Undeterred by the grim silence, she began bringing out more steaming mugs, and Undine used the distraction to slip out of the room, out of the house and away into the icy air.

CHAPTER TEN

Wisps of gray cloud drifted across the surface of the pearly moon. Undine felt the magic surging in waves; it racked her body until she heaved, almost vomiting, but it was without purpose or intent: no magic could take away the memory of the expression on Trout's face. Why had Dan kept pushing? Why couldn't he leave it alone? Dan didn't know anything about the feelings she had for Trout.

Last summer, in the Bay of Angels, she had grieved for Trout; she had breathed air into his lifeless lungs and failed to revive him. She had listened to his body and heard nothing, no pulse, no breath, not even the faintest echo of life. Of course it hadn't really been Trout. When the magic drained away, it was a fish she'd been trying to revive, one she'd accidentally turned into Trout when she had searched for him and found only handfuls of empty seawater. Needing desperately to find Trout, she had unconsciously conjured a copy of him from a fish's body—that was the way the magic worked, as if governed by the same laws as dreams.

Regardless, for her, for a time, Trout had been *gone*, and the grief had torn her to shreds. She had literally lost herself to *loss*: the permanent, unyielding fact of it.

She could not love him, not the way he wanted her to. But his life was precious to her; she could never communicate to anyone how very much she valued his beating heart.

She sat on the stone wall at the lookout, gazing over the flat black river to the scattered lights of the Eastern Shore's suburbs. She sat, but she was restless; her spirit was restless. It was at times like this she found it hardest to suppress the magic. Strong emotions brought it on, yes, but also her will to fight it left her, and her promise to Lou seemed empty and pointless.

The night stretched away from her. The stars began to dissolve, as if her vision was blurring. But it was quite the opposite: her senses were heightened. *Touch*, the feel of the cold air on her skin, of the scratchy stone wall through her thin jeans. *Sight*, the grainy particles of darkness, and inside each particle the composition of space—proton, neutron, electron; matter and antimatter—she could see it all. *Sound*, the waves of sound from the diminishing party, the rustle of the slight breeze in the grass, the silvery tinkle of the gum leaves whispering against each other, and far off the *lap lap lap* of the river. *Smell*, the scent of eucalypt and ice; the faint dusky scent of the native possums and bandicoots and the sharp acid stink of feral cat piss. *Taste*, the taste of snow at the roof of her mouth, carried from distant currents of air.

Her mind drifted upward, into the dome of the

sky, skirting the stratosphere. Snow is always there: residing in clouds are crystals of ice. Mostly the ice dissolves in the troposphere, before anyone can observe its presence. It was not creating something from nothing, to make it snow. It was only a little magic, just something minor, just letting what is *become*, to reach its full potential.

The landscape around her began to change. Her bleak heart, her bleak spirit, filled the air and covered the hillside, blanketing it, *blanking* it. Undine hushed the earth with snow; she made the sky dance with it. Part of her sang, to use the magic again. The bleakness leaked away, and she was left with a kind of bliss, but an erratic, ecstatic bliss that was almost alarming, and made her heart thump against her ribs until they felt bruised black and blue.

She did not hear Grunt coming. "Snow," he said. "Are you doing that?"

It stopped, flakes suspended in midair. "I didn't. . . ." stammered Undine. "I was just . . ."

"Wow. I didn't actually think you were." Grunt

reached out with his fingers and plucked a snowflake from the air. It melted in his hand. "It's beautiful."

"It's a trick," Undine said, angry with herself, and the snow collapsed into water, evaporated into a fine mist, disappeared back into the sky to dwell hidden in the clouds.

Grunt sighed, apparently sorry to see it go. He sat beside her.

"When I was a little kid," he said, reminiscing, immune to the strangeness of the magic he had just witnessed, "it snowed in Hobart. Not just on the mountain, or the foothills, but right down to the beaches. There was snow on the Tasman Bridge. . . ." He waved his hand at the distant illuminated bridge. "I remember seeing people skiing down it on the news. It was amazing. My dad found a big plastic tray, and we sledded down the hill near our house, him behind, me sitting between his legs, steering his knees. It was the best day. And Mum, she lay down in the snow while Dad held the baby—that was my sister Izzy—and made an angel. She got wet, her hair got wet, icicles clinging to it, like she was the snow angel. I've never seen snow like that again." He looked at Undine. "Magic, do you think?"

Undine said nothing. She stared at the bridge, and at the lights winking on the Eastern Shore.

"I like to think it wasn't. I like to think it was something else, just earth, just nature. Maybe God, even."

Undine nodded. She wondered, in a world with magic like hers, was there room for God? She had never really believed in God. There didn't seem any point in it, and he just seemed so, well, *unlikely*. But now, a world that definitely had no God at all felt kind of . . . empty. It wasn't really God she wanted; it was the possibility of God.

"Prospero said you'd stopped doing magic."

"I have."

"But tonight . . . ?"

"It happens more easily when I'm upset." She glanced at Grunt, whose face was impassive, unreadable. "You should know that."

Grunt nodded. "I remember."

They sat quietly for a while. Then Grunt said, "So tell me, how does it go? I mean, you leave Prospero and the bay, you come back to Hobart, to your normal life, but man! Everything's changed. How do you just take up where you left off?"

Undine sighed. "I don't know. That's what I'm trying to figure out." She thought about school and her exams. What was the point of them? What would she do when they were finished? She thought about her relationship with Dominic. She was trying to be an ordinary girl, to fit in with the world around her, but it was as if the space she had once occupied had changed shape—or she had changed—and they no longer fitted each other.

"Maybe you don't go back," Grunt suggested. "Maybe you can't."

"Maybe." She knew Grunt was right. There was no going back to what she had been before. But she wasn't sure she was ready for the alternative—and what was the alternative? Being an entirely magical girl? Where would that lead her? Away. Away from the people who loved her: Lou, Trout . . . she looked sideways at Grunt. She didn't want to be alone.

She tilted her head back toward the party. "Is Trout all right?"

"He will be. You know, Dan . . ."

"I know," said Undine. "He was just protecting his brother."

"I was going to say, Dan's a dickhead."

Undine smiled.

"You should do that more often," Grunt said.

Undine turned to look at him and realized that she rarely met his eyes. She was afraid of what she might see in them, of what he might see in hers, all her feelings revealed.

Grunt said softly, staring into her eyes, "I remember the walk up the hill. With Dad, on that day. It seemed so far, and so hard. We took it in turns to carry the tray, and it was big and awkward and kept slipping in my hands, knocking against my knees. But it was worth it. We slid down that hill, bumping on stones concealed by the snow. It was so fast, I've never traveled that fast in my life, not since. No roller coaster, no car, no rocket to the moon can go that fast. It was scary, but I was safe, with my dad's legs wrapped around me." He held up his own hand and looked at it, and Undine looked away from his face, relieved to be released from the intensity of Grunt's locked gaze. "I remember the shape of my hand, how small it seemed on my dad's leg, how strong he was." He swiveled his hand to and fro, looking from the back of it to the cracked map of his palm. "It was like magic that day. It was rare and it was precious and it glittered like sunshine."

Grunt laid his hand down, and it covered Undine's.

"Show me," he said softly. "Show me."

She said nothing. She was silent, still. Then, as a gift for Grunt, she sent the magic out into the sky and filled the night with a flurry of snow. It seemed to light the sky and the land. Grunt's face was illuminated; it shone with awe at the crystal-filled sky.

Undine gave herself to the magic. She let it fill her. It was breathtaking. But Grunt's presence, the warm gentle pressure of his hand on hers, kept her grounded, and for once the magic felt peaceful, serene, and *safe*. She was the magic, but she was herself, too. It had never happened quite like this before; she'd never felt so much control over her power. It was as if she had almost found a way to bridge the magic and the girl.

She did not know how much time passed. What felt like much later, Undine cleared it all away, restored the landscape to what it had been, and sent the snow once again back into the sky.

Grunt seemed to come out of a trance. His hand lifted from where it had been touching hers. "Have fun in Greece," he said softly, sincerely. By the time Undine looked up, he had gone.

"Good-bye," she said to the empty air.

CHAPTER ELEVEN

Trout and Dan did not speak in the car on the way home. Trout's head swirled with fragments that he could not piece together: the blank staring eye of a fish, the word *never*, the smell of peppermints and old car, the metallic taste at the back of his tongue, and a sensation that someone was exerting pressure on his lower back.

Lately his feelings for Undine had swung from love to loathing like a crazy pendulum. He understood what people meant when they said things about love and hate being opposite sides of the same coin. But fueling the momentum of the pendulum had always been hope. He hadn't realized how much he had still been hoping, until now that hope was gone. Dan had reached out and strangled hope. Inside Trout anger spat and hissed; he could not look Dan in the face.

Richard would have apologized. Richard would have made the peace; the peace was always more important to Richard than the principle. But Dan would not. He stopped at the house, and as soon as Trout had closed the passenger door he drove off, back to the party, spinning the tires and leaving a burn mark on the road.

The bitch of being in love with the girl next door is that even at home she can't be escaped; there was her house, a constant reminder, crouching over him in the darkness. He wondered if Jasper was there, watching him. The kid gave him the creeps. All little kids did a bit. His own childhood, as he looked back on it, now seemed full of lies and bullies and a general pervasive threat. Quicksand, the bogeyman, Bigfoot, nuclear war. Even the Easter Bunny was alarming: a rabbit of immense proportions who knows where you live. Grown-ups that control you. Bad dreams that won't leave you alone.

Trout let himself in. Mrs. M. called down the stairs, "Trout? Dan? Is that you?"

"It's okay, Mum, we're home," Trout lied. "Go to sleep."

He heard her feet scuffle across the hall and their bedroom door close. She wouldn't have closed the door until she heard them come in.

Trout's head was still not clear. He tried to push away the fluctuating anxiety that kept threatening to come upon him; he was sure that if he gave in to the fear that he could not breathe, it would come true and lead to a genuine asthma attack.

He stood at the closed front door. An overwhelming weariness came over him and he rested back, allowing the door to support his weight. His legs buckled under him and he slid down to the floor, sitting on the cold slate in the hallway. The night played itself back to him. He shook his head, trying to clear the images from his mind, but whenever he closed his eyes he could see the fish he believed he was becoming.

He pulled himself up from the ground and walked into the study, stumbling slightly against the wall. He flicked on the computer and connected to the Internet. He typed the Chaosphere's address into the browser.

A quote came up on the screen: *Chaos is process rather than state, becoming rather than being.*

Trout looked at the time. It was 3 a.m. What were the chances that Max would be online? It was months since he'd entered the Chaosphere.

He typed his user name and password. His name appeared in the list of members currently online. Trout's heart skipped a beat. Max's name was there.

He opened a private box.

TROUT: Max, I need to talk to you.

The cursor blinked. Trout waited, but there was no response.

TROUT: Max, are you there? I need to ask you something.

Trout waited. Max didn't respond, but Trout kept typing, desperately filling the blank void of the box.

TROUT: Please. Please. The magic. I need to know. Does it belong here? Do you think it belongs here? In this world? In this universe? Is it natural? Is it real? Should it be here? I need to know.

He knew he shouldn't be here. He knew he was breaking his own rule and putting Undine at risk of discovery by talking about the magic. What would happen to her if people knew what she could do? But his frantic need for answers made him reckless.

TROUT: What I mean is, does magic belong in the universe like sparrows and rice and collapsible garden furniture? Should it be able to act, to save people, to change the future or the past? I need to understand it. Should it be allowed to change things? Should it be here? SHOULD I BE HERE?

In the "members online" list, Max's name suddenly disappeared. Trout put his head down on the desk. He wanted sorrow and rage to tear through him, to erupt out of him in huge raking sobs. But crying wouldn't come.

Why couldn't he cry? He suspected that if he was alive, it was only half a life. Like Prospero, was he destined to spend his remaining years remote from the people around him? Is this what happened when you came in contact with the magic? Did it consume you from the inside, did it empty you out, did it leave you broken and barren? Was he less human, now that he had traded a fish's life for his own?

Before he logged off, he grabbed the pack of sticky notes from the desk drawer. "Chaos is process," he wrote. "Becoming . . . being . . ." He went back to his room. He held the quote up against the wall on the Chaos side, then tried it on the True Chaos side—as if it was a painting and he was trying to find the best light for it. Eventually, in the margin between the two sides, he fastened the scrawled note to the wall.

He peeled off the treacherous green shirt and lay down on his bed. But of course, even there he found no peace. It was a long time before his racing mind quietened enough for him to sleep, and when he did it was fitful: he relived the moment of his own death over and over.

Baby. Here comes the dark.

Though Undine took great care to slide the key silently into the lock and enter the house on tiptoe, it was for nothing. Lou was awake, waiting up for her.

"Was it a fun party?" Lou asked.

"Um. Yeah." Thinking about Trout and the events of the party, and then of course her own broken promise, Undine failed to be entirely convincing. "I'm tired, though. I think I'll go straight to bed." She couldn't bring herself to look at Lou; she felt she wore the magic about her like a gaudy costume, all colors and sparkles and loud noise. She could still feel the aftereffects tingling in her fingers and toes like pins and needles, racing through her blood like pure caffeine.

But Lou seemed distracted, and Undine realized she hadn't been waiting up for her after all.

"Anything wrong?"

"What? Oh, no, I'm fine. I . . ." Lou looked at the cordless phone, lying on the table in front of her. "I had a call from Prospero tonight."

"Everything all right? We're still going, aren't we?"

"Yes, yes. I'm just . . . I'm still not used to him being in our lives, that's all."

Undine sensed there was something more, but she was anxious to retreat upstairs to the solitude of her room. She murmured good night and walked away, her face still cast downward, avoiding her mother's eyes. She lay awake a long time, thinking of Trout's haunted face, the gentle pressure of Grunt's hand on her own, and remembering what it had been like to fill the world with snow.

It was early afternoon by the time Trout woke. His mouth was dry and woolly from the beer he had drunk. His arm was pressed against his face and his skin smelled faintly chemical.

He pulled himself out of bed. The curtain was open, and he went to shut it. Undine was on her balcony, and it seemed she had been watching for him because as he approached his bedroom window she waved. He waved back. She signaled to him to meet her at the bottom of the steps. He hesitated, then nodded weakly. He rummaged on his floor for clothes, passing over the crumpled green shirt where it lay—duplicitous and conniving on the bedroom floor—for his regular uniform of black.

Undine was sitting on the bottom step waiting for him. He sat a few steps up and put his head down between his knees.

"How are you?" she asked tentatively.

"Fine," Trout said to the ground. Then he looked up and managed a sheepish combination of a grimace and a grin. "Did anyone ever tell you that drugs are bad?"

"So why . . . ?"

Trout shrugged. "Why did I take it? I don't know. I guess, just because. Maybe I'm sick of being Trout. Good old predictable Trout."

"Do you remember everything about it? Do you remember what you said to me?"

"I remember what *you* said to *me*."

"But Trout," Undine said, scuffing her foot on the step. "You knew that. Didn't you? I mean, isn't that why you've never asked?"

Trout looked at a far-off distant point, a trick he had taught himself as a kid when he knew he was going to cry. "Yeah. I knew."

"So what about the other thing? About the fish? Do you remember?"

Trout shook his head no, but would not meet Undine's eye. He didn't want to talk about it with her. He couldn't tell her about the dreams. He couldn't tell her that every night she came for him, that every night she pulled the very life out of him.

Undine said, "You must know that it wasn't meant to be you." Trout was silent. Undine went on desperately, "It *wasn't*. It was just a fish."

"It feels like . . ."

"What?"

Trout found he needed to say it out loud. "Sometimes I think . . . it's like the fish died in my place, you know? Like I should be dead, and he should be—"

"It."

"What?"

"*It. It* should be. Not he. It's just a fish."

"Whatever. It should be still there, alive, in the sea. Like I've taken something I shouldn't have."

"No," said Undine. "No, Trout. You're meant to be here. You have to be."

"How do you know? Why?"

"Because . . . because it would break my heart. . . . You're my best friend."

"Yeah, I know. And you're mine. Sort of."

Undine flinched.

"Well," said Trout matter-of-factly. "I am in love with you." It was the first time he'd said it out loud. "I am. That complicates things. It means there's a part of me that will never be your friend. That will never be happy with friendship alone."

"Dan said the same thing last night," Undine said.

Trout nodded. "Besides," he added. "I'm not sure it's a good enough reason."

"What?"

"That I'm here because you want me to be. I'm not sure that's reason enough to cheat death."

"You didn't cheat death. If it hadn't been for me, you would never have been there. I put you in the situation in the first place."

Trout shook his head. "No. God, you're so *arrogant*. You didn't force me. I have agency, I have a mind of my own. I chose to be there. And, just sometimes, I think it should have been me. That I should be dead. That's all."

"That's all?" Undine was close to tears.

"That's all."

Trout got up to go.

"It was just a fish," said Undine, really crying now. "Just a stupid fish."

Trout stopped, but he didn't look back. "It *was* a fish," he said. "It was life. Now it's nothing."

CHAPTER TWELVE

The sun. Old fire burning. Caster of shadows, illuminating difference, speaking an ancient language of presence and absence, light and dark, having and lacking.

Trout hated it. Even in winter the sunlight in Hobart was bright and blinding, blazing through the thin, icy atmosphere. When the sun shone, he felt he could never belong. The world of the day was less and less his, as if by some rule of the universe he had forfeited light and color and warmth when he had dodged death.

In the daytime, Trout seemed to be holding his

breath, his lungs tight and tense. When night came, shadows blanketing the world, Trout began to breathe again. Blackness spread through him, but if you didn't fight the blackness, he found, if you let it take you, then you became something else. Something part night, not completely alive. The sharp edges of the harshly sunlit world were blunted, numbed by darkness.

In the night, Trout walked.

Sunday nights were always the quietest. The air seemed reverent. The cold drifted around him and the river docks smelled like fish and old seawater. He walked down Hunter Street, lined with restaurants and warehouses, the art school on one side and the gloomy water on the other.

He stood under a streetlight, looking at the flat surface of the river, slick and black as oil. He wondered what was below the water, what murky life thrived here. He shivered as the wind bit through him.

• • •

Trout was not alone in the dark.

The girl stood at a distance and watched. He was the one; she was sure of it now. But she couldn't rush things. She had been waiting for too long to mess it up now.

As she watched, she suddenly wondered if he was going to step into the water. Would he sink like a stone, slip away from her? Afraid for him, she stepped forward involuntarily, just as he stepped back. Her movement seemed to have caught his eye; he turned his head and stared straight at her, like he was reading the dark. Her heart leaped, and for a moment she was afraid *of* him.

When his gaze averted, she turned softly, quickly, and walked away. Her heart still drummed inside her. Soon, she promised herself, and excitement coursed through her. Soon, his secrets would be hers.

Trout thought he saw something at the corner of his eye. That was happening to him a lot lately, but usually in the daytime. It was a side effect, he knew, of sleep deprivation. A cogent internal voice told him he needed sleep. But his nighttime wanderings were part of his survival now. He felt it, in a blind, animal way.

Walking home, he felt for the second time that night the creeping sensation at the back of his neck that he was being watched. He whirled around, his coat flapping uselessly at his sides like the broken wings of a bird. Nothing. No one.

A sudden vision of Jasper's narrow, wolfish eyes pressed against his temples. "Big, bigger, biggest, and I will follow you." But it was ridiculous.

Trout laughed out loud. The sound of his laughter echoed in the street, and Trout was surprised to hear how crazy he sounded, even to himself.

He hurried toward home. Maybe when Undine was gone, propelled across hemispheres, he would be able to sleep without dreaming. Maybe he could find a way to reconcile his life—his death—and be whole again, breathe the sunlight and sleep. Sleep. Sleep.

When he closed his eyes, his head swam with sleep. He was exhausted. But as soon as he felt it overtake him, he would force himself awake.

He stopped at his front door and looked up at Undine's house. She's in there, he thought. Sleeping, dreaming, breathing. Suddenly he wanted to slam his fists against her door, to drag her out of bed, to shake the sleep from her. It was an urge so powerful and so violent that it literally rocked him; he staggered and almost fell.

He pushed the feeling away, pushed it deep, strangled and squeezed it, and hid it inside himself. But as he reached his key to the door, he saw that his hand was shaking, and he had to clasp it in his other hand to hold it still.

CHAPTER THIRTEEN

For someone who was only going away for four weeks, there seemed to be a lot of good-byes. Fran said it seemed like extra good-bye because Undine was going to a whole other country.

"Will you write to me?" she said on the last day of term as they walked up to the school buses. "Will you pack up Greece and send it by international courier? Will you take me with you? Will you find me a Grecian god?"

Dominic was predictable enough. "Don't find any Grecian gods," he said with mock alarm.

"I won't be looking," Undine assured him. The last

thing she needed in her life was more boys, even of the god variety. Especially of the god variety. The straightforwardness of Dominic was his most desirable quality. She kissed Dominic good-bye, but the image of Grunt flashed into her mind as their lips touched. Imperceptibly she shook Grunt—and poor unfortunate Dominic—away.

She hugged Fran.

"It's not fair," Fran wailed. "In two weeks we'll be back at boring old school and you'll still be in Greece."

Dominic held on to her fingers. "Don't stay away too long," he said. Undine smiled, already a million miles away.

Trout was the hardest. He had arranged to come to the house the morning of the flight to collect the keys and say good-bye. He was late.

Jasper, persuaded that being dressed was a requirement for international travel only with the judicious application of chocolate, careered around the house with his arms out.

"Zzzoooom," he said.

"Bugger," Lou said to Undine. "I've used up half the plane chocolate. Remind me again why I am taking a three-year-old across the globe?"

"Because you love me."

"Do I really love you that much?"

"Who wouldn't?" And Undine twirled, showing off all sides of her lovableness. She was excited. She wanted to put on her backpack and sit at the front step ready to go, like a little kid on the first day of school.

Finally Trout arrived. He still looked like he needed serious mending. Undine sighed and her bubble deflated, just a little.

Lou swept him around the house, talking a mile a minute. She showed him all the idiosyncratic bits, like the leaky roof in the laundry, the temperamental laptop that Trout was welcome to use, the heater that had to be turned on twice in order to work, the television that made a high-pitched squeal if the color contrast was too high, and the extractor fan that had a habit of turning itself on mysteriously and noisily in the middle of the night.

"You can't actually turn it off," Lou said apologetically. "It just . . . *decides*. Though randomly hitting the buttons sometimes helps." Suddenly doubtful, she said, "You will be all right, won't you?"

"I think I can live with a possessed extractor fan," Trout answered dryly.

"Lou! It's Trout! Besides, his mother is hollering distance away."

"I'll be fine."

Jasper said, "I'm going in a plane." His arms were still outstretched.

"Lucky you."

Jasper stared at Trout and added, as though it were crucial to the moment, "I know how babies are born. The mum goes like this"—he screwed up his face with effort and pain—"and then it comes out."

Trout smiled weakly.

Later, when they were alone, Undine suddenly worried, "*Will* you be all right?"

"Heater on twice, color contrast down, and keep hitting buttons on the extractor fan until it stops or I go mad. I think I can manage that."

"You know that's not what I meant."

Trout shrugged. "I'll be okay. Anyway, you'll be having the time of your life, no time to worry about me. And you're only going for four weeks. Nothing much is going to change while you're gone."

"Come on!" shouted Lou from the bottom of the steps. "Taxi's here."

"Wagons roll," said Trout, which was a dorky thing his dad said at the start of every long car journey.

"Wagons roll," said Undine, and she touched his hand good-bye.

Trout watched Undine leave. He would miss her, of course he would: he would ache with missing. But mostly he was relieved to watch her go. For just four weeks, it would be a reprieve.

She reached the bottom of the stairs, and for a moment she paused, glancing behind her absently as if trying to remember something. She was looking not at Trout or at the house but just at midair, so her face tilted downward, giving the impression of an acute but fleeting sadness. Trout felt strangely compelled to take a mental photograph, summoning all his senses to capture that Undine: distracted, vulnerable, as if she were caught in the precise instant of departure. He had the inexplicable feeling that with their good-bye they would enter into something fixed and utterly binding, and that he might never see Undine again.

The doors to the taxi slammed shut. Undine leaned out the window.

"Good-bye!" she called, waving both hands.

Trout waved, and his smile was wide, generous and sincere. "Bye!"

When he went back inside the house on the steps,

the air was already different, still and soundless as if the house had been unoccupied for years.

Prospero was waiting when they arrived at the airport.

"My daughter," he greeted her, crusty but affectionate, and Undine hugged him. Years of disuse meant his body did not surrender itself easily to her hug, but eventually his old, skeletal frame yielded a little.

"Prospero," said Lou. Her lips tight, she added, "You look well."

It was the kind of thing grown-ups always say to each other, but nonetheless, Undine found it odd, for in Prospero's case it was not exactly true. He was looking older than when she had last seen him, frailer, his skin an imperfect fit on his bones.

"Louise."

Prospero nodded his head gruffly at Jasper; he wasn't used to young children. Jasper leaned closer into Lou but beamed the toothy grin they all called his "best smile."

It was the first time Undine had seen Prospero in a public place, and it seemed to her that he was not quite real compared to the other travelers, almost as if he were a fictional character come to life.

When they took their seats on the plane, Prospero had trouble doing up his seat belt. Undine reached over him to help him, and Prospero sat back, compliant and helpless as a child. Or rather, more helpless and definitely more compliant: across the aisle Jasper fastened and unfastened his seat belt several times until Lou shoved what looked like the rest of the plane chocolate in his mouth. As the plane taxied down the runway, Undine noticed Prospero's hands were shaking, almost imperceptibly.

"You okay?" Undine asked softly.

Prospero slipped his gnarled hand into hers without answering. His skin was not what she expected—she thought it would be dry and cool like peeling tree bark. But instead it was warm and alive, and the warmth traveled into her own skin and up her arm and into the core of her.

Suddenly the plane accelerated, speeding down the runway until it reached the velocity it needed to lift off. They rose into the air, the ground falling away from under them. They swung around and traveled over the dry interior of the island. As they left the sea behind them, Prospero's grip tightened.

Undine watched the collage of fields, rivers, mountains, towns, and lakes pass beneath them. The plane was still climbing. They reached the first wisps of clouds and the land beneath began to dissolve. As they ascended into the thick stratum of cloud, Undine was struck by this thought: that the land was disappearing, vanishing altogether, and that when they descended it would be into nothing, into nowhere, and that the world she knew would be gone.

CHAPTER FOURTEEN

At bedtime Trout realized that Undine no longer shared his hemisphere. But still he was surrounded by her. Her room looked as if it was still in the process of being left, with clothes scattered on the floor and the chair. He lay facedown on the bed and inhaled. The bedclothes were infused with her warm spicy smell. He smelled it in his dreams; he tasted it when her lips met his.

Lou had not told him which room to sleep in, and in the end he chose no room, or rather sleep did not choose him. As if married to his old patterns, when darkness came, he went out.

He went up the steps to Camelot Drive instead of past his own house. It was cold and clear. From the high point of the road he could see across the city, across the river to the Eastern Shore. Hobart was surrounded by hills, and coming down Camelot Drive into the city, he had the impression that he was descending into a hollow place, into the navel of the world.

Occasionally he would pass a house and a burst of noise or light would suddenly assault him: televisions and stereos, domestic disputes, a baby crying. But mostly the city was synchronized; it slept.

At the end of Camelot Drive, where it forked with another road that led into the town center, there was a pub with a rather seedy reputation. Trout never went inside pubs. He did not intend to go into this one, but something caught his eye: a glimpse of white-blond hair, a familiar angular feminine face.

He stood at the doorway, peering through the dim, smoky light. A lot of kids from school came here; they would serve anyone and never asked for ID. Tonight there was a band playing. The music was not the sort Trout normally listened to, but it was quite good, sort of smoky and grungy, with a strong melody and not much beat.

He looked for the girl he thought he had seen, but there was no sign of her. He didn't know whether to be glad or sorry. She had broken down the rules of the game; he had stopped behaving randomly: he had come looking for her twice now. It unsettled him.

He found himself at the bar. The bartender raised his eyebrows in question. Trout looked through his pockets. He had no money. He was about to leave when he heard a voice behind him.

"Hey, Trout, baby! Can I get you a beer?"

It was the chicken-bone girl, minus her bone. Her presence was alarming. It felt like a setup, like a joke, like a mean cosmic joke. He looked around him. He wasn't sure how to act now, how to restore randomness. It was only in making random decisions that Trout felt he maintained some control over his own life.

The way to bring back randomness was to do the opposite of what he expected himself to do. So he let the chicken-bone girl buy him a beer. Now that she no longer had a bone in her hair, he realized he needed something else to call her, so he asked for her name.

She laughed. "Jeez, you were out of it the other night. Eliza."

"Lize!" shouted a guy at the pool table. At first Trout thought that he was accusing Eliza of lying. "Lies!" But it was apparently Eliza's—Lize's—go.

"Come on, Trout. Be my lucky charm."

Trout followed her as if he had no will of his own. Maybe he didn't. He sipped his beer cagily.

Eliza circled the pool table looking for her shot; her eyes were sharp. With the long cue held up to her side, she looked like a hunter.

She made the shot. The balls ricocheted off the white ball and each other, several of them slipping down into the side pockets.

"What do you know?" she said. "Looks like you are my lucky charm."

Trout didn't want to be anyone's lucky charm. He put his beer down and waited for Eliza to have her next shot before saying, "I might go."

"Go?" Eliza said. "But you just got here."

"Yeah, I wasn't planning to stay. I was looking for someone."

"Not me?" Eliza stuck her bottom lip out in an exaggerated pout. She was playing with him, Trout knew that, but he didn't know how to play this game.

"You haven't finished your beer. Dell, tell him he has to stay and finish his beer."

Dell grunted.

"You better do what the lady tells you," said the other guy. "She's into voodoo, this one. She might turn you into a toad."

"Into a fish," said Eliza. "Isn't that right, Trout?"

Trout's heart started pulsing. "Why did you say that?"

Eliza looked at him. "Because of your name. That's all. Chill out."

He heard them laughing; he knew to them his

behavior seemed bizarre. He tried to calm himself down. Nothing was going on. It was just coincidence. *Synchronicity*, said a voice inside his head. *Magic.*

"It's not magic," he said out loud. "It's just chaos." Patterns of order in apparently disordered systems. Science. It was a statistical probability that he would run into her; it was the law of averages. Hobart was a small place. There were rarely more than a few degrees of separation between any two individuals in Tasmania. You sat and you compared friends, relatives, music teachers, primary schools, and eventually you'd find a link. It was a parlor trick, a party game.

"What?" Eliza said, sniggering. "What did you say?"

Trout realized he was muttering. But as she spoke, she filled his head again. *Magic*, said his head. "Shut up," he said. "Shut up. I can't think."

Suddenly he was convinced she was somehow responsible for the pattern that was emerging where before there had been simple chance. She had given him the drugs on the weekend. Some voodoo thing?

Some magic? Had she poisoned him? Possessed him. He looked at his beer. Had she done it again?

His heart was racing. His breath choked in his throat.

"What have you done to me?" he gasped.

Eliza put her hands on her hips. "Listen, mate, I didn't do anything. You're weirding me out, all right?"

One of the guys came around the table with a pool cue in his hand. "I think you better step outside."

Trout pushed past him, out into the clear night air. He pushed hard, he didn't see the guy fall clumsily against the pool table. He inhaled rapidly. He forced himself to control his breathing, concentrating on each breath. What was happening to him? He leaned over, his hand on his knees. He didn't see that he had been followed out of the pub.

From the dark back corner of the bar, the girl watched Trout. That boy really needs a good night's sleep, she thought.

From where the girl sat, she could see Eliza bend to take her next shot and finish the game, pocketing the eight ball. By the time Eliza stood up, her male companions were gone. Eliza smiled slyly, and chalked her cue. She racked up the balls, and waited.

Despite the fact that he was being punched in the head, Trout smiled.

He fell to the ground. The stars seemed close; they moved, danced like fireflies in the black sheet of the sky. Now he was on the ground, they stopped using their fists. They kicked him for a while, Trout could not tell for how long or how hard. Then somehow they disappeared. Trout didn't see them go: by then his eye had swollen and he could see little at all. But he was quite sure they had left, because they weren't kicking him anymore. He lay there for a while, drifting in and out of consciousness. All his life he'd avoided being beaten up, and now he couldn't see why. It was kind of magnificent, really, except for the excruciating pain.

• • •

A few minutes later when the boys returned, the girl at the bar rose. As she passed Eliza, she said in a pleasant, even voice, "You're done. If I ever see you near him again, I'll kill you." Eliza's sneer froze on her face and became the parody of a sneer, a cheap imitation.

When she walked past the boys, one of them whistled. She stopped. She struggled with herself and did nothing.

"Dyke," one of them heckled.

Neanderthals. She kept walking.

Trout heard a sharp burst of melancholy music, and lucidly he realized someone was opening and shutting the pub door. He heard a soft footfall. He looked up and saw a girl with white hair, rimmed with gold like an angel.

He heard from very far away the sound of his own name. The sound rippled around him, as if the girl were speaking underwater. He could almost see it, silver on the air.

He peered up, trying to focus on her. But the world wheeled with colors, blending away into white, into light, and Trout was gone.

Before he opened his eyes, Trout could smell something warm and sweet like oranges and cinnamon wafting through the air. His eyes drifted open, or at least, his eye. The other was swollen shut. It was not completely sealed—he could force it open—but it behaved badly. The room swam out of focus, and his stomach lurched as if he might be seasick.

The room. With his one good eye he studied it. There was a wooden dressing table with a mirror covered in jars, pots, and bottles of gels and sprays and lotions and creams. Girl stuff. The citrusy smell was a candle that burned brightly by the bed. The curtains were white and wavy; there was a faint hint of rosy gold light behind them—dawn.

He tried to rise, pushed himself up on the bed. His head throbbed; his arms gave way underneath him. He closed his eyes. Just resting them.

When he woke again, the curtains had been drawn. The light that came in from outside was bright and blue—Trout guessed it was midday. The candle was out, and soft music murmured through the door's cracks.

Trout felt worse than before. His whole body throbbed. His torso felt bruised, but on the inside, and if he breathed in deeply, pain wrenched through his ribs. Cautiously he prodded his left side. Ouch. But not too ouch. He didn't think anything was broken.

His hands traveled up to his face. He felt around his eye. The swelling was alarming, as if a whole second face had been grafted onto his. Remembering the mirror, he hauled himself to sitting position. He shifted down the bed so he could see.

All around his eye was thick and black. His cheek was swollen and bruised, and his lip was cut. He swiveled his head. The left-hand side of his face was fine. He looked like some kind of evil clown or something, a character from a kid's book. Normal one side, deformed on the other.

He glanced around the room uneasily. Where was he? He remembered, vaguely, a girl. Was that who had brought him here? What was she doing? Flitting in and out, lighting candles, drawing curtains. Why did she bring him here and not to the hospital? He called out, "Hello?" His voice came out a rasping cough. He tried again, and though his voice was clearer, there was no response.

He pulled himself to a standing position, using the bed end for support. In the mirror, with his tall frame hunched over, his one good eye and one bad, he suddenly reminded himself of Prospero. The mirror held him in its gaze and Trout stared back, horrified. He seemed to see his true self: aged and broken, as deficient and derelict as the old man.

He staggered to the doorway, his hands outstretched and fumbling, more falling than walking. His hands found the door, and he propped himself upright against it for a moment. He edged sideways so he was supported by the door's frame, and with one shaking hand he turned the handle.

He knew where he was straightaway. The curtains that he had peered through from the outside were now flung wide open to show the garden, and beyond it the sloping and rising hills of rooftops and houses, on one side going down to the river, on the other undulating up the mountain.

From above the top of the armchair, he saw her feathery hair, white as porcelain, as a bone bleached in the sun. She seemed to feel his presence. She turned around.

"You're awake."

Her blue eyes looked upon his injuries. He felt an impulse to cover his misshapen face, but he didn't; his hands stayed resolutely by his side. She stood up. She was as tall as Trout, thin and bendy like a birch tree. Those sapphire eyes, they seemed to Trout to be hardly human.

He almost heard what she was going to say before she said it; her words filled the air around him. Her head tilted, she seemed to hear it too, like the whisper of falling leaves.

"I'm Maxine Madden." She smiled apologetically. "But, of course, you know me as Max."

Part Two

TROUT AND MAX

CHAPTER FIFTEEN

Maxine Madden had a love-hate relationship with Tasmania. Hobart was beautiful to look at, the view was captivating, you could get lost in it. People did get lost in it; in the mountains, they disappeared. Whole human beings vanished.

Max had been fifteen when her father went missing on Mount Wellington. He had flown down for a weekend's bushwalking with family friends and never returned. Tasmania was foreign to her then; it was Narnia, Terabithia. It was an imaginary land where people went on driving tours and fishing trips and sometimes didn't come home.

Now she lived here: Max, who for three years hadn't lived anywhere, who as soon as one city, one country, began to recognize her face had shifted to the next.

Every morning she looked out her kitchen window and—when the day was clear—the first thing she saw was the blank, velvety face of Mount Wellington, almost close enough to touch, as if she could reach out her fingers, rummage around in the trees, and pinch her father off the mountain's side. Mount Wellington, with Hobart pinned to its skirts, seemed such a domestic little thing. But there it was. You took the wrong turn and then the weather set in and suddenly it turned on you. Her dad had been wearing shorts, a T-shirt. They said he probably wouldn't have survived the first night, definitely not the second.

Maxine had prayed that there hadn't been a second. The thought of him somewhere, cold, lost, injured, and *living through the first night* only to perish on the second, it was more than fifteen-year-old Maxine could bear. Or twenty-year-old Max, for that matter, which is why she had taught herself not to think about it.

They had brought something out of the mountains, a week later. They rang her mother. Maxine heard her mother say, "You found him?" and hope had flickered alive in her chest.

But they had found only the husk of him, an empty, cold, lifeless shell. It wasn't her father, because her father's hands were always warm, his eyes crinkled at the corners like he knew a secret joke, he was strong, he could lift Maxine high off the ground and swing her around.

When she realized that she would have to come to Tasmania to find the answers she was seeking, she had laughed out loud. It was such a strange twist—it almost made you believe in fate. This was why she loved chaos. It acted on all of them; it was the governing law of the universe.

That mountain, it was there now, peering in through the window over Trout's left shoulder. She moved slightly so it was out of her view, the mountain's inscrutable face fully concealed by Trout's.

She expected surprise in that face, astonishment, maybe even delight. But he looked at her as a teacher might look when admonishing a willful pupil: disapproving, almost disappointed.

"How did you find me?" he asked quietly. "You've been following me?"

"No! Oh, well, once. Twice. But I had to be sure."

"That night at the docks. That was you?"

Max nodded. "Last night at the pub was the only other time."

"Were you following me last night? I thought I was following . . ." He eyed her warily, as if he were rethinking what he'd been going to say. "You still haven't told me how you found me. Are you from here, from Hobart?"

"No. Last year, after you logged on to the Chaosphere and told me about the storm, I found this." She went to the top drawer of a desk in the corner of the room where her computer sat. She handed Trout a computer printout. FREAK STORM CATCHES WEATHER WATCHERS BY SURPRISE. "I was in . . ."—she tilted her head and thought about it for a moment—"Belgium, maybe."

He looked at the article and gave it back to her.

"It took me a while, in libraries and Internet cafes, sifting through newspapers, studying weather patterns, to narrow it down to Hobart. But once I did, it was obvious."

"But how did you find *me*?" His voice was deliberately low and even, giving nothing away.

Max had brought Trout here, to her home, thinking it would give her some power over him. But it wasn't working out that way; he was asking the questions, she was on the defensive.

"I used a virus." She said it with no trace of apology.

"You infected my computer with a virus?"

Max waved her hand. "Nothing that will hurt your computer. It just records your keystrokes. So I could read what you write, what anyone writes on your computer. I learned it from hackers I hung out with in Berlin. They used it to get credit card numbers off the Net."

"Sound like a swell bunch of guys."

"What makes you think they were guys?"

Trout shook his head. "What about the other night? On the Chaosphere. I did come back, looking for you. But you didn't *answer* me."

"No."

Suddenly Trout realized, "That's when you were installing the virus?"

Max nodded, her face impassive, unreadable—but definitely not sorry.

"I was *begging* you," Trout said hotly, then immediately embarrassed. "I needed you. I thought you were my—"

"What? Friend?" Max seized control, more brutally than she intended.

Trout shook his head wearily. He realized how naive he sounded.

"Some friend! We talked to each other twice," Max said. "And then you disappeared. You told me something earth-shattering—*universe* altering—and then you just disappeared! I waited and waited for you." The last statement sounded pathetic to her ears. She shook it off. "The magic. I needed to know more. You don't understand how important it is to me. There's so much it could do. . . . I was standing on the precipice of the most important discovery of my life. And then you just . . ."

Trout couldn't remain unaffected by the desperation in her voice. He recognized it—he had felt it himself, that urge, that drive to know the magic, to know it utterly. "I . . . I wanted to come back to the Chaosphere sooner," he admitted. "I wanted to tell you everything; you can't know how much I longed to share it with someone. But don't you see? I couldn't. The risk . . ."

"The risk," Max stated. She met Trout's eyes. "You were right to be afraid."

"What?"

"I'm not the only one who's been waiting for you."

"But how could they . . . ?" Trout realized. "You told other people about me? I trusted you!"

Max felt herself lose her poise. "You trusted a *stranger*! I thought it was nothing . . . a hoax. At first I thought you were making it up."

Trout held her gaze. She shifted uncomfortably.

"No, you didn't," he said. "You knew it was for real."

"It doesn't matter," she pleaded. "I know I shouldn't have told them. But you don't understand. You don't know what the Chaosphere is. . . ."

"A bunch of freaky teen witches. Isn't that what you once said?"

"Some of them, mostly the ones in the chat room. But would I be there if that's all it was?"

"How can I believe anything you say? The only person who's come after me is you."

"The only person?" Max said pointedly. "What about last night? Look at yourself."

"They weren't anyone. They were just . . . no one." Trout was confused. Eliza's face, mean and sharp and sly, entered his mind. "Weren't they?"

Max shrugged. "It's an Internet site. How would I know what they look like?"

Trout's sore head was pounding; he was finding it difficult to concentrate. "But how would they even find me? Unless you . . ."

Max shook her head. "I haven't told anyone where you are. But if I can infect your computer, then they can."

Trout still looked skeptical.

Desperately, Max said, "I can prove it. The virus. I can show you the one I used to enter your system, and we can see if they've used one as well."

Trout thought, then shook his head. "The computer is at my house. I don't want my mum to see me like this." He touched his face and flinched.

Max shrugged. "So we'll have to sneak in. Tonight, when they're sleeping."

"You mean break in? To my own house?"

"Well, it's your house. So it's not really breaking in. Just . . . sneaking. Like I said."

Trout wasn't sure he could see the difference.

"You want proof, don't you? You want to know if anyone else is tracing you?" Max persuaded. "Please let me do this for you. I need to show you; I need you to trust me. I need the magic . . ." she faltered off, looking pleadingly into Trout's eyes.

"The magic?" Trout asked. "Why? What do you need it for?"

Max faltered. It struck Trout as strange. It was after all an obvious question for him to ask and she'd had time—days, weeks, months even—to come up with a slick response. And yet the question made her seem . . . lost. He almost felt sorry for her, but a wave of wooziness overcame him, and he concentrated on feeling sorry for himself instead.

"Okay," Trout said reluctantly. "This doesn't mean I trust you." But his anger was ebbing; tiredness overcame him.

"Do you trust me enough to sit down?"

"Not really." But he did anyway; he staggered from the door to the couch. In the time it took Max to cross the living room, boil the kettle, and clean two coffee cups, Trout had fallen into a fitful but dreamless sleep.

Chapter Sixteen

The Ionian sea glittered beguilingly at Undine. She stared at it, entranced. It was still early, dawn streaking rose-red across the sky, but the day promised heat. She thought about suspending herself in the sea, letting herself drift. . . .

"Going swimming?"

Undine jumped, and Sofia smiled at her. Sofia had met them at the airport early this morning when it was still dark. After giving Prospero two European-style kisses, she had greeted Undine, Lou, and Jasper in a broad Australian accent. She had grown up in Melbourne, but every Melbourne winter, one of

Sofia's parents returned to Corfu to run the Domatia—the hotel where Undine and her family were staying. Sofia had just finished her uni degree and so this year had come to Greece with her mother, Lena, before backpacking around Europe. She casually dropped names that made Undine's heart spin: Venice, Istanbul, Prague—fairy tale cities bejeweled with possibility.

Sofia had told them all this as she drove aggressively through the crowded center of Corfu Town and then continued north to the tiny village that would be home for the next four weeks. Prospero had prearranged everything with Lena, who Undine thought might be some kind of distant cousin or something. Jet-lagged and weary, she hadn't followed the conversation very well. But Lena had been delighted to see Prospero and he had been equally pleased—in his reticent, stern way—to see her.

"Coming for a swim?" Sofia said again, nodding her head sideways at the water, as though it were not the most stunning view she'd ever seen. "The water's great. Warm from the summer. And kind of . . . buoyant. I think it's the salt content."

"Sounds incredible," Undine said, and she couldn't keep the tone of longing out of her voice. "I . . ." But looking past Sofia she saw Lou standing on the other side of the unsealed road from the beach, just in front of their hotel. "I can't," she said regretfully to Sofia.

"Oh, well. If I can't tempt you . . ." Sofia shrugged and walked down to the water.

Lou crossed the road to join Undine on the loose surface where road became sandy beach. She snaked her arm through Undine's. "Looks great, doesn't it?" Lou said.

"Don't worry," Undine told her, feeling harassed by Lou's intrusion. "I'm not going to swim."

Lou looked at Undine, sharply. "We don't even know if this sea would affect you the same way the bay did. The bay has its own magic."

But Undine could feel a familiar low hum resonating from the water, not as loud and overpowering as in the bay but still present. She glanced at Lou. If Lou was magic like her, wouldn't she feel it, too? But Lou didn't seem to; she was watching Sofia kick herself off and lazily swim out toward the rising sun.

Undine sighed. She tried to forget Lou beside her and the promise between them that threatened to drag her back to her everyday, complicated life. Instead she gazed around at the landscape that surrounded her.

The village was small and peaceful, with white, ochre, and dark pink houses built up a rocky hill overlooking a natural crescent-shaped harbor. The light and the air were somehow whiter than at home, and it was almost as if she could see it, as if the air was composed of a fine white dust. Though now, as dawn spread, the whiteness colored into a blushing apricot.

Lou tugged gently at Undine's arm. "Let's go in and have some breakfast, maybe get some sleep." As soon as Lou said it, Undine realized her mind was buzzing like a badly tuned radio and her skin felt greasy and gluey from more than twenty-four hours in transit. Even outside in the fresh air she felt a little sick and light-headed from the lack of sleep. Her knees were sore from sitting for so long on the plane.

Inside Lena had laid out a large breakfast of bread, cold meat, cheese, and fruit. There were also small pastries like doughnuts, soaked in honey. Jasper ate about five of them until his eyes began to blink slowly and Lou took him off to bed.

Undine let herself into her own room, between Prospero's and the room Lou shared with Jasper. She lay on top of the cool, fresh, clean sheets and closed her eyes.

Four weeks, four glorious weeks, stretched ahead of her. It was her chance for a true holiday. No school. No mournful Trout or hazardous Grunt. Just fun, sun, and—she smiled—two parents, the full set. She was just any girl now. She turned her head to look out at the beach one last time.

The Ionian sea glittered and danced in the early sunlight. Being "just any girl" meant no magic, she told herself firmly. Which meant no sea. She closed her eyes again and let sleep drift over her, to the tune of the music of the waves.

When Trout woke, he was alone. Dusk was settling on the rooftops outside. The curtains inhaled and exhaled, breathing icy mountain air.

Panic seized him, making his chest tight. What was happening to him? All of a sudden the disparate, chaotic elements of his life were colliding, grafted together like some kind of hideous mutant plant.

He thought back to the first time he had seen Max, here at her flat, in the yellow light of the driveway. Could that have been planned, too? Certainly the next time when he had peered through the crack in the same curtains that billowed toward him now, she had not had any say in it. She couldn't have sorted through his brain, told him what to think, how to feel. Could she? His instinct was no. But if it was not Max who had arranged things, then who? Was someone else messing with his life? Was it the chicken-bone girl, was it voodoo, was it magic? Was it death itself? He felt hunted, hunted by . . . what? Chaos? Chance? Fate? Or by Max, simply by Max?

He couldn't get his head to clear. Nothing made sense. How had she brought him here? He'd been unconscious. She must have had help; she was wiry and tough-looking, sort of resilient like a bendy willow tree, but not strong enough to carry a whole person by herself.

On the other hand, she *was* offering proof. She said she was trying to protect him. And, he admitted to himself, he wanted to believe her, that her intentions were good. Perhaps if there *was* some higher power, some interfering, interventionist trickster of a god, then Max was like . . . an angel: ministering, guiding. Or perhaps merely—selfishly—Trout was relieved to find someone to share the magic with, someone who wasn't Undine.

"You're up."

She was standing at the door looking at him.

"I'm up."

She was, he thought reluctantly, quite striking, with her sinewy leanness. Her feathery white hair framed her arch face and arctic eyes; she looked like a snowy owl. He didn't *need* another improbable girl in his life, another complex, dizzying, unpredictable element of the female variety.

"Tea?" Max offered.

It was sweet and strong and poured down his dry throat as luxuriously as liquid gold. They sat opposite each other at a small square table in the kitchen. Trout eased his limbs into a different position, with little gain—his skin was raw, his joints and bones ached, and the pain in his side was sharper with every inhalation.

"So," Max began casually. "About the magic . . . ?"

"I still don't trust you, remember? I'll tell you when you've proved to me I can."

Trout saw a fleeting greedy look pass over Max's face. But she looked deeply into her tea, and her face smoothed until it was quite void of emotion.

Max dished out rice and thick puddles of brown curry. Trout mopped his plate with flat bread. The food churned in his belly; he was nervous about taking Max to his home, and about the possibility of Dan or his parents seeing him as he was, beaten and bruised.

He was also feeling suddenly, ridiculously shy. Apart from Undine, he hadn't spent much time with girls. He knew he should still be angry with Max—even frightened by her sudden appearance in his life—but he felt he already knew her from his secret observations. Plus he felt a little guilty: although she had clearly intruded on his life, he had intruded on hers.

They left the house just before midnight, setting out through the slumbering streets. It was surreal to have someone walking beside him. It was almost as if he had dreamed Max up, as if the night had made her out of ice and air.

Where Undine walked below his shoulder height

and looked up at him, Max, her hands dug into the pockets of a short black denim jacket, was at his eye level. He was in pain, his left side still burned; nonetheless he walked at his usual pace, and Max with her easy, cervine gait had no trouble matching it.

"You know," he said, thinking of Undine, "you haven't asked me about . . ."

"'I'm going to sing you a song, but I'm not going to tell you about a girl.'"

"What?"

"Nick Cave. In *Wings of Desire*. Then the music starts and he says—"

"'I'm gonna tell you about a girl.'"

"You know it?" Max smiled. "I love that film."

"Me, too."

They walked in silence. Trout said, "But I'm not going to tell you about a girl."

"I know."

"Not yet."

Max looked at him, met his eyes. "Trout?"

"Yes?"

"I'm really sorry I didn't talk to you that night."

"What night?" Trout asked, sharply. He had been thinking back to that first night, weeks ago, when he had seen her outside her own flat, her hands cupped over her mouth, her eyes leaking tears. He felt suddenly ashamed that he had been there to witness that private grief, and that he hadn't intervened, stopped those girls from writing whatever it was that had hurt Max so.

"The Chaosphere. Last Saturday," she clarified, studying his reaction curiously. Trout closed his eyes in a long blink. Of course. "When you asked me . . . what was it? If the magic was natural? If you should *be* here. Something else happened, didn't it? More than just the storm?"

Trout shook his head in reply, but he didn't mean *no*. It was more that he was trying to shake the fog from it.

He was still having trouble making connections, like trying to do a giant puzzle where you knew there were going to be pieces left over at the end. He didn't know how to make the picture of his life whole and complete; he didn't even know which pieces belonged to him and which pieces were just part of the background color: the sky, the field, all that jagged blue, that jagged green, filling in the spaces around him. And if they didn't all belong to him, then which pieces belonged to someone else's jigsaw puzzle, which pieces were someone else's jagged blues and greens?

When they got to his house, it was dark and quiet.

"We can't go through the front door. Someone might still be up," Trout whispered. He thought for a moment. The house would be locked tight.

Max's eyes traveled upward. "What about that window?"

Trout looked up. His bedroom window was open a crack.

"But how would you get up there? Don't tell me you can scale walls."

"The tree." There was a big old gum tree with several sturdy limbs that grew to the left of Trout's window. "Haven't you ever climbed it? It's a perfect climbing tree."

"Not for years." He looked down at his useless, battered body. "I don't think I can. . . ."

Max appraised the tree. "I can get up there, no worries. Is there some way I can let you in? A back door or something?"

"There's a door in the laundry. Down the stairs, and through the kitchen. You have to jiggle the handle; it sticks. But be careful. My brother might be up. And sometimes my father has trouble sleeping."

"He doesn't sit up with a big gun across his lap, whistling through his teeth, does he?"

Trout tilted his head as if he were considering it. "Not my father. But based on recent behavior, it sounds like a step up for Dan."

"Great." Max observed the tree, then grabbed the lowest branch and tested it with her hands, pulling down to see if it would bear her weight.

"I can't believe you're doing this," said Trout.

"I used to do gymnastics at school."

"Well, that's good, then, right?"

"I sucked at it."

"Oh."

"They taught us how to fall."

"I would have thought 'don't' would be about all you'd need to learn on falling."

Max laughed, and Trout liked the way she looked when she did.

"Here goes nothing," Max said. "Any last-minute advice?"

"Don't fall?"

"Ha-ha." And then Max grabbed the branch with both hands and pushed herself up. Trout could see muscles tightening under the skin. She swung her legs over and stood up gracefully, balancing to reach the next branch. It was hard to imagine her sucking at anything. "Hey," she hissed. "This is fun."

"Just be careful."

She ascended easily and quickly. The tricky bit was covering the distance from the tree to the windowsill. Trout remembered the year Dan had fallen attempting it, collected fortuitously by the branches of the tree so that the incident only resulted in a broken arm. Had he fallen in another direction . . . Trout shuddered. It had never occurred to him before how close a shave that had been for Dan.

Max now inched outward from the heart of the tree. The branch she was on bent and creaked, and Trout heard the sickening sound of snapping wood. "Max!" he whispered fiercely. "Get back! We'll find another way." But she didn't hear him, or didn't acknowledge him if she had. In his mind's eye Trout saw her fall as Dan had done all those years before.

"Tada!" Max stood on his window frame, one arm outstretched, singing softly. Trout clapped soundlessly, but he let out a long exhalation of relief. He watched Max slip through the window.

It occurred to him that he had just been an accomplice to an almost complete stranger breaking into his own home. Now she was inside and he was locked outside—was he crazy? Quite possibly.

Max appeared at the window. "Hey," she whispered. "Meet you at the laundry door!"

Trout waved to indicate he'd heard her, and Max disappeared.

Max watched Trout leave. She went to his door and pressed her ear against it. Silently she opened the door and tiptoed to the top of the stairs. Someone was still up, the television murmuring, light flickering in the hallway. She hesitated, and suddenly the light disappeared. The television had been switched off.

Quickly Max retreated back into Trout's bedroom. Her eyes readjusted to the darkness of the room. Looking around her, she could see the walls were covered with paper, but it was too dark to see the images and words on them. She flicked on Trout's bedside lamp, and the soft glow illuminated the images and text—a gallery of chaos.

The Trout Max had talked to online nine months

ago was a very different person from the Trout she had met tonight—the Trout who had decorated his room in this way. Last year Trout had been driven by scientific curiosity, but tempered by his feelings for his subject. He had asked the right questions, and Max had considered him bright but naïve. The way he bolted when Max had probed him for more information had been frustrating but not, she had realized almost immediately, surprising.

But this Trout, he was truly haunted.

Entering his room was like entering his brain, and, she thought with a shock of recognition, it was almost like entering her own brain. She read the quotes and looked at how he had put his work together. *Chaos* and *True Chaos* read the headings. She knew what that meant—some chaos scientists used "true chaos" to describe a state where the laws of chaos didn't apply, where there truly was no order, no pattern, just randomness and volatility. So Trout, Max supposed, was questioning whether magic had some kind of guiding principles or whether it was truly random, meaningless, a gesture from the void, from nowhere, from nothing.

She looked around his room again. It was, she thought, kind of sexy to be inside someone's brain, especially when their brain was as wild as this.

She heard footsteps coming up the stairs. Quickly she leaned over and flicked off Trout's lamp. A door opened and closed. She breathed heavily, savoring the sense of excited anticipation at almost getting caught. A few seconds later a radio hummed. She crept out into the hallway and down the stairs. She peeked in through doors as she passed them and noticed the study, the computer dark and silent. She kept going, through the kitchen, into the laundry. Behind the closed exterior door she could hear Trout's rasping breath. She pressed her cheek against the door for a moment and listened, before turning and softly creeping back to the study, her fingers curling around the cold metal disk in her pocket.

• • •

Trout seemed to be waiting a long time. He tried to pace through it in his mind. How long would it take for her to tread softly down the stairs, through the kitchen, and into the laundry? When he was quite sure she could have done it all five times over, the door in front of him began to jiggle.

"Boo. Did you miss me?"

"What were you doing?"

"Rifling through your stuff."

"Very funny."

"Someone was moving around downstairs. I had to wait."

"Who was it?"

"Your brother, I think. He went into the bedroom opposite yours and turned the radio on."

"Yeah, that would be Dan. Okay. Let's do this quickly."

He led Max into the study. Trout went to sit down.

"It will be faster if I do it," Max hissed. "I know what I'm looking for."

Trout knew she was right, but he stepped aside

reluctantly. She flicked on the computer, taking control. "Wow," she said, sitting down. "This is a really crappy system."

"Thanks. I like to think so."

"No wonder I didn't have any trouble penetrating your firewall."

She didn't seem to have any trouble breaking into anything. Trout wondered briefly if she wasn't a little morally . . . lacking.

She clicked through files and folders rapidly. Trout watched dizzily, unable to keep up. His mind raced, trying to remember what documents of his were on there. What personal, private . . . ? But it was a shared, family computer. There was nothing private about it. For the first time he was grateful he didn't have his own. If he did, he was sure Undine's name would be plastered all over it, in the same way that it occupied every spare corner of his mind.

Even so, he looked at Max sideways. From his essays to his parents' tax records to his father's letters to Great-Aunt Glad in Arkansas, it was the bones of his family laid bare, to Max and to anyone else who had accessed their system. Max had invaded not only his computer but his private life, his personal stuff, and his family, as sure as if she'd sat down to dinner with them while rifling through Richard's CD collection and wearing his mother's hat.

"There," she said. "Found it just where I left it."

"Shhh!" Trout heard footsteps coming down the hall. They both froze. Trout tiptoed to the door. "It's my dad. He's gone into the kitchen."

She pointed to two viruses she had isolated in his system. They appeared as innocuous folders embedded deep in the program files directory. Trout leaned over to look. One was called, simply, *Max*. "This one's mine," she breathed, her face close to his. Her breath was warm and tickled his ear canal pleasantly. Focus, Trout, he told himself sternly. She pointed at the one called *ChaosSystem*. "That's them." She pulled a disk out of her jacket pocket. "Antivirus," she whispered.

"You want me to . . . ?" She waved the disk.

"No. I'll do it." Trout wanted desperately to regain control. Sitting here, seeing Max's name on his computer, it was a shocking reminder that she was also MAX, and now she was here in his study like a cyberghost, as if she had not entered by the door—or by his bedroom window—but had traveled through wires and networks and binary code to get here.

"It will take too long. You don't know the codes."

"Okay." As uncertain as he was about Max and her motives, Trout felt violated at the thought of more people digging around inside his computer. He felt he had no choice, in this instant, but to trust her. "Just do it."

"It'll take a while."

"I'll keep watch."

From the study it was just four soft steps to the kitchen door. From there he could see his father standing over the kitchen sink. Mr. Montmorency had a glass of water in his hand, but he didn't drink. He stared out the window into the darkness.

He looked ashen and gray. Insomnia again, Trout supposed. Feeling like an intruder he retreated, stepping backward, but under his foot a board creaked.

"Trout? Is that you?"

Trout jumped. Instinctively he covered his bruised face, though in the hallway he was concealed by darkness.

"I thought you were staying at your girlfriend's place up the steps." Trout didn't answer, but his dad went on anyway. "First Richard, then you. Dan'll be next. You know the best thing about having kids, Trout?" He paused to drink his glass of water, downing it in a few gulps. "Seeing them grow up. You know the worst thing?"

Trout shook his head, though his dad couldn't have seen him in the dark.

"Seeing them grow up." Trout retreated further. "Trout?" Mr. Montmorency's voice was unexpectedly frail, questioning the dark. But Trout didn't answer. He hated leaving his father in doubt like that, thinking he'd been talking to shadows, to no one, to nothing.

The study was unexpectedly black; the computer had been switched off. At first Trout thought Max might have left, that the night had swallowed her. Or that she was at large, roaming the house. Then his ears picked up the faint sound of her breath, fast and shallow. His eyes picked her out, a shadow in a room of shadows. She was by the window, pressed against the wall.

"We have to go," hissed Max. "We have to go *now*."

CHAPTER SEVENTEEN

It was early afternoon when Undine woke, starving and disoriented.

She sat up and pulled on her clothes, and was about to open the door of her room when she heard voices, first Prospero's, then Lou's, high-pitched and angry. She stood at the blue wooden door, pressed against it, listening.

"All I meant," Prospero was saying, his aged voice soothing but firm, "was that you should consider the possible outcome of having Undine make such a promise. You can't control—"

"But don't you see?" Lou broke in. "I *can*. I can

control the magic. I've always been able to. Except when *you* seduced me into using it."

"But you *can't* control Undine. Lou, she's more powerful than either of us, than both of us together. You don't know what will happen if she's not encouraged to—"

"I expected this from you! You don't care about Undine, about your daughter. The magic always comes first."

Prospero's voice was subdued. "You know that's not true, Louise. You know how much I *do* care about Undine."

"But it's too dangerous! It's too reckless; there's no place for it in Undine's life. She needs to learn to suppress it. It's the only way she'll ever be happy."

"Louise. Those months when you were with me. You were happy. After everything your parents put you through . . . it was wrong of them to make you turn away from who you are."

"Everyone's *wrong*, aren't they, Prospero? Everyone

except you. Haven't you ever wondered if maybe it's you that's wrong, your obsession . . ." Lou stopped. When she started again her voice was thick with tears. "Happy? You think I was happy? You could never make me happy, not truly, Prospero. I was . . . *drunk*. On magic. I wasn't happy."

"Louise . . ."

Undine shifted against the wall. This wasn't what she'd hoped. She didn't expect Prospero and Lou to fall in love again; the very idea was absurd. In fact she found it impossible to imagine that they had ever been a couple, let alone had a baby together. But she wanted them to like each other enough that she could have a family: a weird, dysfunctional, broken family, but still one that could get together for birthdays and Christmas without . . . without *this*.

"Louise," Undine heard Prospero say, "I made a promise to you. No magic, for me or Undine. All I ask in return is that you think about what I've said."

She heard Prospero leave and Lou sigh. Undine

stood conflicted, wondering if she should confront her mother, when Jasper's high, excited voice suddenly filled the room, accompanied by Lena's soft contralto. Relieved, Undine waited till she was sure Lou had gone before she let herself out into the flagstone courtyard. Lena was sitting out there, staring at the blue sky, sipping a coffee as thick and black as treacle.

"Hungry?" Lena asked, as if she had been waiting for Undine. "You must be." Without waiting for an answer, she disappeared into the kitchen and came back minutes later with a bowl of steaming soup and rice, thick with egg, flavored with lemons and garlic. It was filling and nourishing and Undine felt less strange and light-headed when she had finished it.

Lena directed her down to the beach where Lou and Jasper were playing. "Jasper has already made a friend," announced Lena proudly, as if she had cooked up a suitable playmate in her kitchen with the same speed and skill with which she had produced the magnificent soup. Undine almost believed she could have. "Your father has gone walking in the village."

Standing outside the hotel Undine saw Lou and Jasper playing with a girl with long brown pigtails and a bright green swimsuit. Lou waved, and Undine waved back. Jasper and his friend waved, too, Jasper so vigorously that he fell backward onto the sand, but Undine kept going. She wasn't ready to talk to Lou yet. She wanted to see Prospero first.

She found him sitting on a bench at the pier, watching fishermen spread their nets out to dry. Pegged to a line strung between two lampposts were several squid, their long legs dangling in the warm air like washing hung out in the sun.

"Ew."

Prospero smiled. "I remember scenes like these from when I was a boy." He patted the bench beside him. "I've never kept up with the world very well; it seemed to transform so rapidly. It is reassuring to see that things don't always change."

Prospero pointed out what he could remember. "See that house?" He gestured. "A famous English author lived there. My father used to drink whiskey with him on Sundays, and he let me read his books. And there, the village square. We would play football there, and the women would come to fetch water from the fountain and gossip and give me grapes and figs and sweets. And there the men would sit in the evenings and drink ouzo and flick their worry beads. . . ."

Undine was enjoying hearing Prospero talk about his childhood. It made him . . . *fit* more precisely in her life and made her feel like she was part of something bigger than herself—a family stretching backward through time.

"Tell me about your parents."

"My mother was Greek; she was born in this village. You're a lot like her."

"Was she magic? Like me?"

Prospero smiled. "Undine, no one has ever been magic like you. You're alone in the universe." His voice was proud, but Undine felt a tight, uncomfortable knot form in her chest when he said it. "She was magic like . . . well, perhaps like your mother. When I stood close to her, I could hear it inside her, like listening to the echo of the sea inside a shell. Things happened around her; her garden always flourished, as if the soil was whispering to her and she was whispering back. She could cool the earth with rain—a light shower, nothing like your storms—or part the clouds to bring the sun. She hid it from my father—she knew it would frighten him—but never from me. Perhaps she thought a child doesn't see, or perhaps she wanted to teach me. . . . When she was close I found I could do things, too, small gestures. That was when I learned to tame the wind—I made a pet of it, small whorls of air that could carry dust and seeds, and capture butterflies, and . . ."

Prospero sighed, and hesitated. His face had been golden and joyous as he remembered his mother, but now he turned to face Undine. "You must understand, I was a boy, brave and reckless. My father caught me, playing at my mother's skirts—I was only a few years older than Jasper—and she was laughing at my games. He was English, and though he loved my mother, he never really understood her Greekness, her religion and her superstitions, her strange customs, her family's intrusive and passionate ways, and now this. . . . He hated the magic, he hated especially seeing it in me. So I was sent away where he wouldn't have to see me anymore, sent to live with my grandparents in England." He shrugged. "They loved me in their way. Or at least they loved the English boy they tried to make me become. My mother died soon after I left her." He held Undine's hand tightly. "When I was a boy, I thought my mother had died because I had been taken from her. That she had died from a broken heart. Now I think perhaps she was broken, but because my father would not let her use her magic.

"Your promise to Louise. I understand it, I

understand her fears for you, but it worries me. It is a dangerous promise, to put away your magic, to let it simmer and seethe inside you. It should be given form. It should be allowed to sing. In this way only will it become something beautiful. Things that grow in the dark are dark themselves."

Undine felt torn. She looked pleadingly at Prospero. "I can't break my promise to Lou. I can't. Anyway, it's only for a year. I told Lou I wouldn't use the magic till I finished Year Twelve."

Prospero squeezed her hand. "Of course it is. Only a year. Now," his voice brightening as if he was ready to change the subject. "What else can I tell you? That house there, that is where the American girls lived, two of them with long plaits on each side of their heads. They were very naughty girls; they taught me to swear. And there is a track up behind"—his finger searched the landscape—"that house. It is a steep walk, on a donkey track, up through the olive grove. We would go there and find things for ourselves and our mothers—flowers, tortoises, mushrooms, old clay pots and tablets and beads. Such a magical place, so ancient. Old forgotten stories buried in the land, fragments of people's lives lost long ago."

Undine gazed up the hill. "Is it far to walk?"

Prospero shook his head. Undine stood. "Want to come?"

"I am a happy old man, sitting here."

Undine sat down again beside him. "You're not old."

"I feel old," Prospero said, speaking out to sea. But seeing her worried face, he smiled. "I'm just tired. But you go."

"Are you sure?"

Prospero nodded, his eyes drifting out to sea, to the horizon, beyond it, again.

Undine made slow progress up the slippery stony path. A herd of surprised goats regarded her curiously as she tried to maintain her footing and gathered hurriedly to one side, protesting loudly to one another about her presence. But the climb was worth it. The air was warm and sweet and the hillside was thickly populated by butterflies—they brushed against her skin and landed occasionally on her shoulder, her bare arm, or in her hair.

She sat at the top of the hillside by a tiny church, only big enough for one person to kneel in. From here the view was overwhelming, sweeping right across the village and the bay. Far to the left, at the outskirts of the village, she could see Lena's hotel, white and blue against the rocky cliff face behind it and the brilliant sky and sea beyond.

From this vantage point, alone on the hill, far above her family and with great swathes of air, sea, and land between herself and Trout, and herself and Grunt, Undine allowed herself to fully feel her remoteness. For half a year now she felt she'd been living every aspect of her life from a great distance, that when she spoke what might sound to others a quiet murmur, she was in fact shouting over a deep and dark crevasse, and when she touched, though she might appear quite close, she was actually teetering perilously over the same chasm, reaching to her very limits.

She had hoped that perhaps in Greece the feeling would leave her, that she would feel more bound to her family. But already she floated beyond them somehow, not anchored like they were—Prospero by his memories, Lou and Jasper to each other.

She closed her eyes. The magic tugged, like an eager child wanting to lead the way. What was it the magic wanted to show her here, in this ancient landscape, this place of history—history of people, history of her? Did she dare let the magic out . . . and if she did, could she drag it back in?

Lou said it was dangerous to use it; Prospero said it was dangerous not to. Undine no longer knew what to believe. Last year in the bay it had almost overwhelmed her; she had almost destroyed everything, even herself. But she hadn't in the end, had she? And what would happen if she didn't allow the magic to grow and develop? Would it eventually overwhelm her? Was she stronger than the magic she contained? Was she more girl than magic, or more magic than girl?

As she thought, she allowed herself to feel it inside her, the sensations she lived with and ignored every day. The magic was like giant swirling loops, like a golden, fizzing lasso made from the sparks of an exploded firework. It jerked and swooped and arced inside her.

Was she the magic, or was she the girl? There was only one way this question could be answered and that was to let the magic out. Holding it in, keeping it back like a dog on a tight leash, would never reveal anything about its true nature. She held the question in her head and suddenly, sharply, she gave the magic a little flick—releasing it, but immediately jerking it back in, like a fishing line.

At once she realized that in releasing the magic she was releasing herself—she had been so tied up, so bound by her promise to Lou, that it had begun to strangle necessary parts of her: now her heart beat easily, her breath flowed freely. It was similar to the peace she had experienced by Grunt's side as she had filled the night sky with snow, but this time the feeling was far more powerful. Her body was flooded with bliss, prickling the tips of her fingers and toes like pins and needles, true and joyous and entirely encompassing. But with it came too a surprising pain, a dragging, clawing sensation that began deep in her guts and pulled violently upward as though it might actually wrench her into pieces.

Then something happened to the world around her; she felt the shift that meant the magic was working beyond the boundaries of her body. (Briefly she imagined the curves of herself—her hips, her lips, her eyelids, her ears, her breasts—as parentheses, encapsulating her body as a series of asides, digressions, afterthoughts.) She opened her eyes.

From the landscape she watched herself form, a girl with a skeleton of stones. Her flesh was earth, packed tight around the stone bones. Finally the girl was covered in a living, swirling skin of butterflies.

Undine watched, fascinated and appalled. The goats bleated nervously and retreated down the hill, tumbling over each other and their own bony ankles, skittering sideways. She reached out her hand and the girl—the Undine made of stone and clay and painted wings—reached out her own fluttering, flickering one, but before they could touch, the butterflies dispersed into the air and the girl crumbled, falling to pieces back into the land.

Undine was left reaching to an empty space, and the emptiness echoed inside her, knocking against her hollow ribs.

On the beach Jasper and Olivia dug deeper and deeper in the sand, until the bottom of their hole filled with seawater.

Jasper said, "If I was a crab, I would get my pinchers and cut your hair like this, snip snip."

Olivia squealed and grabbed her pigtails.

"What would you do if you were a crab who was a boy?" she asked delightedly.

"I am a boy," said Jasper. "I am a crab who looks like a boy."

"I am a seashell, curled up and quiet," said Olivia. "I am a sea horse, and under the sea I ride like this." She showed Jasper.

"My sister is a girl, with butterfly hair."

"So am I," said the girl.

"No, you're not," said Jasper. "You're a sea horse."

"I am so a girl. You're a crab."

"I'm also a boy." Jasper looked at Olivia for a moment. "You can be a girl," he offered.

"I am a girl." Olivia was getting upset.

To mollify, Jasper said, "Look at this." And like a magician, first he showed Olivia that his hands were empty, palms outward. He closed them together like a clamshell. Then he opened them, and out flew a butterfly, spiraling upward into the empty sky.

"Do that again," said Olivia. But her parents began gathering up their things—towels and bags and beach umbrellas and Olivia's bucket and spade—and told Olivia it was time for tea. Jasper ran back to Lou; he had already forgotten his trick. But even when she was an old, old lady, Olivia never forgot the boy who made a butterfly appear from nothing, out of his hands.

CHAPTER EIGHTEEN

Max took charge. While Trout stood frozen, she eased the study window open and slithered out with ease. For Trout it would be a much tighter fit. He stared doubtfully at the small space. Max's head popped up at the window's gap.

"Come *on*."

"Why?"

"No time for why!" Max hissed urgently. "Just trust me."

Trout stepped cautiously through the gap in the window. His legs dangled uselessly toward the ground.

"Drop!" ordered Max. "I'll help you." She bore his weight as best she could, but Trout still landed heavily, grimacing with pain.

"Can you run?" she said. "We have to go."

"Stop. Tell me what's going on."

"I saw someone, walking around your house in the backyard, toward the laundry door."

Which they had left open! Trout stared, horrified.

"But, my family . . . I can't just leave them. . . . I have to warn them."

"Don't you get it? It's you they're after! *You're* the one putting them in danger." Max tugged his hand. "Come on," she repeated. "We have to get back to my place."

Trout hesitated. He jangled the keys to Undine's house in his pocket. In the back of Trout's mind, there was still doubt about Max. He was wary of giving her such direct access to Undine, to her private space. But he wasn't sure he wanted to return to Max's either. It was a long walk back, and his body was tired and sore from his injuries. All he really wanted to do was let himself back into Undine's house, drag himself up the stairs, and collapse on the bed—to sleep, dreamlessly. "I know somewhere else we can go," he said. He headed toward the front of the house, but Max stopped him.

"It's too brightly lit under the streetlights," she hissed. "There might be more than one of them."

Trout stopped and thought. "There's another way," he said doubtfully.

He led Max through the side garden, keeping a wide berth between them and the rear entrance to the laundry. He was slow and clumsy, his leg dragging a little. Max in contrast was wound up, a tight spring of nervous energy.

He looked back toward the house. There was no sign that anyone was actually pursuing them. There was a light on upstairs—Dan's room. As he watched, another light came on, and another, first in his parents' room, then Richard's. That was odd: Richard hadn't been home at night for months.

"Max," Trout whispered savagely into the darkness.

She appeared beside him; he could not tell from where.

The warm honey light radiating from the house was inviting.

"Let's go back," he said.

"We should keep going," Max said. "There's nothing we can do. We have to keep you safe."

Trout stared at her. "What if they hurt my family?"

"And what could we do? You? Fight them? Look at yourself."

Max was right.

"Look," she said. "When we get up to the road, we'll find a phone and call the police. Okay?"

"Okay."

Trout looked at the rivulet that formed the boundary of his backyard. He could barely see a meter in front of him. "We have to cross this." It wasn't wide; there wasn't much current. But it was too wide to do in one or even two jumps, and Trout knew from experience that the rocks were slippery.

"Is there a bridge?"

"Not for a kilometer or two up that way." Trout felt pathetic as he added, "I'm not sure how far I can walk."

"It's okay. I'll go first."

Max stepped out onto a stone, and almost lost her footing. She peered at the shadows at her feet, then stepped again. Trout heard a splash. "Ugh! It's *freezing*."

"Are you all right?"

"My foot slipped. Oh, god, my shoe's filling with water. This is disgusting." Trout heard her jump again. Finally she said, "I'm over. Just watch that second rock; it's slippery."

As Trout stepped out onto the first rock, it began to rain, just lightly, but it was icy cold and the temperature dropped. A wind with the breath of snow in it seemed to come straight down from the mountain. He shivered.

He shifted his weight and lifted his back foot. He realized then that he wasn't correctly placed for it. There wasn't room for him to bring the other leg onto the first rock; he'd have to leap for the second.

With nothing but blind faith, he propelled his poor, hurting body forward and landed on the second rock. The next jump could either take him to the other side, or he could hedge his bets and go for a third rock. He decided on the safer option. But he felt himself sway forward and almost lose his footing. Just before he jumped, he changed his mind and aimed for the bank, falling short so he splashed through the bitter cold water, drenching his shoes and socks.

Now he faced the treed bank that climbed up to the road. Too steep to build houses on, it was vacant land owned, Trout supposed, by the council. In the dark, in the rain, with a faulty body and the possibility of someone pursuing him, climbing it seemed to Trout an almost impossible task.

Max was apparently making good progress; Trout could not see her but he could hear her scrambling up the bank. Trout pulled himself from tree to tree. The trees were mostly young and flexible, they gave little support; some slipped through his fingers. He was fighting back tears now. It felt to him that his body was in danger of packing up completely. He stopped to rest.

"Trout," Max called softly. It made Trout jump. He thought she had climbed ahead, but her disembodied voice seemed to come from behind him. "Shush."

"I am shush," Trout snapped back.

Suddenly Max was beside him, whispering in his ear.

"Shush!" Max said again, her lips grazing his ear. "Listen."

Trout listened. He heard the rain hitting the leaves of the trees, the trickling passage of the rivulet, Max's soft breathing, and his own, fast and ragged. His ears picked up a swishing sound. It took him a second or two to work out what it was. It was the sound of someone pushing through the long grass on the other side of the rivulet at the end of his garden. He looked down the hill, and he could see through the trees and the darkness an intermittent beam of pale light. A torch. They *were* being followed.

"Come on," Max said, grimly. Trout, fear gripping him, harnessed all his inner resources and began the tortuous ascent again. The noise that he and Max made climbing the hill filled his ears, though he desperately listened for their pursuers. A tree branch dragged across his face and he jumped, thinking it was a human hand.

The hill got steeper, the trees thinned out. He crawled on hands and knees, his fingers clawing through the dirt which was turning to slushy mud. The rain fell steadily, soaking his clothes. His breath came in choking sobs now, though his only tears were the raindrops that fell from the sky and hung to his eyelashes.

Trout was beginning to seriously believe he wouldn't make it when his hands touched not mud but the tarmac of the road. He saw pools of light—the streetlights reflecting on the road's wet surface. Max was waiting for him. "Come on!"

she said, and she grabbed his hand, pulling him upright.

"I *can't* run," Trout gasped, but he did anyway, pulled along by Max. "Max!" he shouted, but his throat was constricted and no sound came out. Her hand, wet from the rain and slippery with mud, slithered out of his and she ran ahead. He called again. "Max!"

She turned. "This way." He led her to the steps. "Halfway down," he gasped. They ran down the steps to Undine's front door. As if in a bad horror movie, Trout fumbled the keys, dropping them on the wet concrete. He scrabbled in the dark to find them. His fingers were numb with cold and when he did find it, he had trouble maneuvering the key into the lock. But finally it slid in, he turned it, and they both fell inside.

Max pushed the door closed, leaning her whole body against it.

"Was anyone coming?" Trout asked.

Max shook her head, eyes wide. He wasn't sure if

she meant no or simply that she didn't know, that she'd been too frightened to look.

Trout was shivering violently.

"You're freezing," Max said, and she stepped forward, touching his cheek. For a moment their eyes met. Max looked searchingly into his face. Trout could feel himself being pulled toward her—it felt like gravity; it felt like science. It was almost out of his control, bodies attracting. . . .

Confused, he pulled away. Disappointment flickered briefly on Max's face. Trout realized with amazement that she *wanted* him to kiss her.

"We both need to warm up," he said, then blushed at his own double entendre.

"I'll turn the heater on," said Max. "You get in the shower."

Trout thought back to Lou's eccentric advice. "You need to turn it on twice." The heater belonged to another time, B.M.—before Max. It belonged to the golden age of Undine, to the era of her benevolent tyranny over his heart.

In the bathroom Trout peeled off his wet clothes. He looked down at his body. Blue, red, and black bruises bloomed down his left side. His hands were torn and bloody; so were his knees. The pain in his side was sharp and stabbing. He eased himself under the lukewarm water with his hand on the cold tap. Every time his mind started ticking over, he tightened the cold tap, blasting himself with another burst of hot water until it was so scalding he couldn't bear it.

Self-consciously wrapped in a towel, he went upstairs to dress. He pulled on navy tracksuit bottoms and a long-sleeved blue T-shirt, dressing for comfort, not glamour. He selected a pair of flannelette pajamas from Undine's drawer, feeling deeply treacherous as he rummaged through her things. Despite Undine's assertion that nothing would ever develop between them, that his feelings were one-sided, he felt unfaithful to her, having another woman in her house only two nights after she had left the country.

Max was waiting by the heater, wrapped in a soft white towel. He handed her the pajamas and went into the kitchen while she changed. He glanced up: reflected in the window glass he saw the long curve of her naked back, before he busied himself again making hot tea and toast.

By some law stranger than magic, Undine's pajamas fit Max, despite the foot's difference in their height. Trout would never understand women's clothes. Max toweled her hair roughly as Trout laid out their victuals. He sat beside her on the couch.

"Are you going to call the police?" Max asked.

Trout had stood at Undine's window, looking down on his house peacefully slumbering in darkness, asking himself the same question.

"What would I say?" he said to Max. "'My best friend is capable of a dark and powerful magic, and now I think some scary hackers from the Internet are after me'?"

"Doesn't really ring true, does it?"

"How is this my life?"

Max shook her head, wearily. "I don't know. But, hey. Thanks for sharing."

"Pleasure's mine."

He leaned back and closed his eyes. "Who do you think it was? Did you see?"

Max didn't answer. And Trout didn't care. He felt sleep wash over him. *Will darkness or light be born?* whispered dream-Undine. "Oh, shut up," said Trout sleepily, and surprisingly, she did.

CHAPTER NINETEEN

Trout woke slowly; he kept his eyes shut for a moment or two as wakefulness swirled inside him. He became aware of a warm pressure on his side. He put his hand to his shoulder and came in contact with a handful of hair. He opened his eyes. Max was snuggled against him, sleeping, her face serene.

He eased himself up without disturbing her and checked the clock on the video. 11 a.m. He had slept for hours. Despite the fraught night's activity, he actually felt rested. He stretched his limbs and winced. Still sore. His face, though the swelling had gone, still stared gruesomely back at him in the mirror, mottled yellowish green and blue.

He went into Lou's room to use the phone, perching on the edge of her bed.

Dan answered.

"Is Mum there?" Trout asked.

"Why do you care?"

Trout was surprised, until he remembered the fight he'd had with Dan. It paled into insignificance after the events of the night before. "Just get her." He sighed.

"She's not here."

"Dad then?"

"No."

"What happened last night?"

"Last night?"

"You know what I'm talking about." Trout had already planned this. He was deliberately casual. "I looked out the window at . . . I don't know, sometime after midnight, and all the lights were on."

Dan conceded, grudgingly. "Someone broke into the study, but Dad thinks he scared them off."

Trout squirmed. "So everyone's all right, then?"

"Yeah. Peachy."

"Good." Trout felt annoyance creep into his voice.

"So bye." Dan hung up.

Trout looked at the phone. "Bye," he said, hoping his sarcasm was a powerful enough force to travel the distance between him and his brother and punch Dan in the nose.

"So?" Max was standing in Lou's doorway, still soft and dewy with sleep.

"Nothing. They're fine. It was *us* that frightened them."

"Oh. That's good, isn't it?"

"That we frightened them?"

Max didn't answer. She was elsewhere, detached.

"Max, who *did* you see last night? Who was following us? Was it the people from the pub?"

Max's face was blank, almost as if she had lost interest. She shrugged. "It was pretty dark. Breakfast? I'm *starved*."

She let herself into the kitchen and began opening

and closing cupboards. Trout felt his anger transfer from Dan to Max. She was making herself at home, nonchalant about the risk to which they had exposed his family—and themselves. Again he had a feeling that she was a bit emotionally . . . blank. She had used a term last year in their online chat: morally neutral. It had disconcerted Trout then, and it bothered him more now, now that she was standing in Undine's kitchen cracking eggs into a bowl.

She looked up and met his gaze. "Sorry," she said. "I'm hopeless without breakfast. And last night . . . scared me." Trout softened. Of course Max had been scared, too. She went on. "I *was* expecting them, but not so soon."

"Expecting who? Who's *them*?"

Max shook her head. "How should I know? Anyone can access the Chaosphere. People who want to do more than study the magic. People who want to . . ."

"Want to use it," said Trout, flatly.

Max nodded.

"What for?"

"Why does anyone want power? For power's sake, I suppose."

Trout looked at her appraisingly. "To help people. To end droughts. To save someone they love from . . ." He stopped, but let his face say the rest.

Max blinked. "Well, all those things, too. But somehow, I don't think they want to make it rain puppies."

"And what do you want to use it for?"

Max shrugged. "I don't really. I just . . . I'm like you. I want to understand it. Take it apart, see how it works."

Trout listened uneasily. He wasn't sure if he believed Max—her tone was too casual, her response sounded too rehearsed. But she'd proved at least that she was on his side, for now anyway.

"So what do we do now?"

Max held up the whisk, twirling the eggy end in the air. "We eat breakfast."

Max's own clothes were still wet, so Trout went upstairs to procure more of Undine's. He came back with some loose, fleecy lined track pants and a hooded windbreaker.

She eyed them doubtfully. "High fashion," she said.

"I didn't think her other clothes would fit you." Besides, Trout thought but didn't say, these were some of Undine's favorite winter clothes and he loved them on her. Nor did he add that as he gathered them from the drawers he had almost felt her inside them, warm, fragrant, soft.

Max disappeared into the bathroom to change. She came back and did an exaggerated model's twirl for Trout's benefit. The clothes hung loosely around Max's body, a little short in the leg, making her look soft and rumpled as freshly dried laundry.

"She's smaller than you." Trout said apologetically.

Max pouted. "You think I'm fat."

Trout's astonished eyes traveled over her lean angular frame. "No! Absolutely no. I just . . ."

When it came to girls, Max suspected Trout hadn't a lot of experience. She let him off the hook. "Just kidding."

219

What was curious was that he was living in a girl's house.

"This is *her* house," she said. "Isn't it?"

"Yes."

She pointed at a photograph of Undine and Stephen that hung on the wall.

"Is that her?"

Trout nodded.

"She's gorgeous. I can see why you two . . ."

"We're not. Well, *I* am. But she's not."

"Her loss. Who's the hottie with her?"

"That's her father. I mean, her stepfather, Stephen. She only met her biological father for the first time last year."

Max looked at the photo with the same envy she always felt when she saw girls with their fathers. "He reminds me of . . ." She caught Trout looking at her. She amended her initial thought; she didn't want to talk about her own father, not to Trout. She didn't want to expose that scarlet thread of damage that ran all the way through her. "He looks nice."

"Yeah, he was."

"Was?"

"He died a few years ago. Undine never really got over it."

"Why *would* she get over it?" Max snapped, staring at the photo a moment longer. She shook herself, remembering Trout. She brought the conversation back around to Undine, to the magic.

"And is this where she made the storm?"

Trout was staring at her curiously. "Outside." He nodded to the backyard.

Max opened the door and stepped into the garden. The sun was out; there was a touch of warmth in the day. Max closed her eyes and stretched her arms above her head, locking her fingers. She breathed in deeply, as if she could breathe in the magic that had once inhabited the air around her. She exhaled in a rush.

"It must have been so exciting. Imagine feeling the power of a whole storm pass through you. Like an electric current. And controlling it, wielding it."

Trout looked uneasy. "It wasn't really like that. It *was* pretty amazing," he admitted. "But scary. She could barely control it."

Max whirled around. "Oh, Trout!" she exclaimed. "What *was* it like? Tell me about the magic!" As soon as she'd said it, she knew it was too soon. Damn it. And she was willing to wait, to give him time to get to know her, to trust her.

His silence was awkward and heavy. She stepped forward and took his wrist gently in her long fingers. "It's okay," she said. "When you're ready."

"I want to tell you. But . . ."

"You don't trust me."

"It's not that. I do . . . I mean, I think I do." Max let her hand linger on his skin.

"You know, it *is* her loss," Max said, and she meant it. She leaned forward and kissed Trout on the mouth. He returned the kiss, tentative and blind, fumbling his lips inexpertly on and around hers. His tentativeness made the kiss all the more arousing; she tasted his uncertainty like sweet, warm wine.

Chapter Twenty

Grunt propelled himself forward, swinging his torch back and forth. This far undersea, it was dark. Not impenetrably, soul-suckingly black or anything—greenish sunlight filtered through the swathes of kelp—but around the wreck it was dreary and dim.

The gloominess didn't bother him. He was used to it. He even kind of liked it, which is why he dived alone, against all the rules of scuba. But this was the way it should be. Just man and nature. It was some kind of primitive code in his DNA, something that dated back to when humans were part of the primordial goop. Or whatever.

So when his torch failed, he didn't panic. He drifted, waiting for his eyes to adjust, as if suspended in a starless night sky.

In the distance, beyond the wreck, something luminesced. He swam toward it. What would have its own light source down here? Most things on earth borrow light from something else, like the moon or sun, or they convert energy into light. But this was different. As he drew closer he felt a strange sensation, tingling from his skin inward. A kind of energy buzzed in him. It *sang*. He swam closer. The light blinded him, so he could only look past it or around it, not directly at it. Whatever it was, it wasn't really an it. Located at the base of a large rock formation, it wasn't an object, it was more a space—or an absence of space—like a crack in the world. Energy spilled out of it; the closer he got, the more he thought he wouldn't be able to bear it. But it wasn't unpleasant. In fact, the feeling that burned in him—it was alien, it was peculiar, and yet it was not entirely unfamiliar.

He turned his face upward to where light played on the surface of the sea. He kicked his legs and propelled his body up, tunneling through water, breaking through the white foam waves and diving into thin cerulean air.

Undine dreamed of the bay. She dreamed the angels were dancing, swaying somberly and weightily from side to side to the night's own song. Undine was there, huge against a September sky, made of stone: stone skin, stone face, stone heart. Trout was also there, more fish than human, silver, reflecting moonlight on mirrored fin.

A slit erupted in her side, tearing her from end to end, spilling light. The moon fell from the sky, into the waiting arms of the ocean; stars whirled into the vacuum of her wound. Or was it the reverse? Were stars born from it, coming from inside her, out?

She half woke—the warm Greek air wafting in through the open window was sweet as honey.

Before she opened her eyes she had the strangest sensation that Grunt was there, beside her, reaching into the core of her most secret self and strumming the magic inside her.

Grunt dragged a hand through his coarse hair as he pulled Prospero's boat, *Sycorax*, out of the water onto sand. Salt water plastered the ends of his dreadlocks to his face.

Ariel barked and ran in and out of the water. She hated it when he went diving. He had left her up at the house but, as always, she'd come looking for him.

"Come on, pup," he said, though the dog was as aged as her absent owner. "Let's go back up to the house."

Grunt wasn't easily spooked, not even when diving alone. He took things as they came, on face value. But even so, he wasn't sure what to make of what he had found that morning. There was something in particular that nagged at the edge of his mind, though he couldn't quite put his finger on it.

Up at the house he used Prospero's phone. Tran, the coordinator of the marine archaeology group, was annoyed. "But it's *perfect* conditions for diving. We've already got the equipment down there. Why would you want to postpone?"

"I can't explain. Personal reasons. To do with the old man who lives here."

Tran expelled air with the force of a combustion engine. "All right. Whatever. Three days. We don't actually need his permission; the wreck's in public water. But you can have three days."

"Thanks. And sorry, man."

He hung up the phone. And suddenly he placed it, the feeling he got when he swam near the light, from the energy that pulsed within it. It was the same feeling aroused in him by the close proximity of Undine.

Trout knew that there had been some powerful kisses in the history of the world, kisses that had changed the shape of things to come. Julius Caesar and Cleopatra. Samson and Delilah. Yoko Ono and John Lennon. A kiss can seize history. Wars can rage in a kiss; battles can be lost and won.

But this was not that kind of kiss.

Max was pleasantly salty and bitter, like an olive. Her mouth was warm and firm, and her lips were soft. But they were still lips, and Trout did not lose himself in them. He tingled pleasantly enough at first, and had the kiss not lingered perhaps he could have been convinced by it. But as it went on, he found himself growing increasingly awkward.

Finally the kiss ended. Max pulled away; her eyes remained closed for a second. Trout stared curiously at her face. Some people were like oil paintings, beautiful from a distance and kind of splotchy up close. But even from this nearness, Max was stunning. Her skin was clear and smooth and flawless. Her eyes, when they finally opened, were startling blue— the same color as a clear seaside day—and her white-blond hair seemed to sparkle with electricity.

Trout could not have imagined someone who looked like Max wanting to kiss someone who looked like Trout. So why did he not particularly want to kiss her? He wanted to want to. Max was an intriguing future for him: she was not Undine; she was new; she was steeped in possibility.

As a scientist, Trout had studied love as seriously as he studied any field of science. Despite his lack of field experience, he knew what a kiss should feel like, and that it had not felt as it should was . . . impossible. Look at her, he said harshly. Beautiful, sexy, lithe, strange. Now look at you, all knobbly knees and Adam's apple and . . . nice (meaning bland) looking, well brought up, boyish. If he couldn't be transported by that kiss, then something was missing from him, something vital.

He couldn't keep going the way he was, caught halfway between life and death. He needed . . . commitment, one way or the other, he needed to know. Was he dead? Was he dead inside? Max was . . . well, she was weird. But she was everything he should want in a girl: adventurous, gorgeous, smart, and . . . and *into him*. That was something he would never get from Undine.

Staring into Max's azure eyes, he realized what it was he had to do. If there was something missing from him, he had to return to where he'd lost it, to where he had last been whole. He needed to stare it in the face—death. It was time to return the bay.

CHAPTER TWENTY-ONE

Still jet-lagged, Lou and Prospero wanted to spend the day at Lena's place or in the village or at the beach, relaxing. But Undine, who had woken early, was seized with urgency. She was struck already by time fleeting; her holiday would slip through her fingers before she knew it and be gone.

"You," grumbled Prospero, "are too young to worry about time."

But he didn't know about the temporary girl on the hillside who had fallen apart. He didn't know about Undine's emptiness. After the stone girl, and her dream about Grunt and the Bay of Angels,

Undine felt she might be temporary, transient, that she herself was in danger of falling into parts, back into the landscape, or seascape, from which she had come.

Lena took pity on her—or on Prospero and Lou—and invited Undine to join her. "Sofia will take you sightseeing tomorrow. But today perhaps you might like to see the town? The markets are busy, and fun to look at for a tourist."

Undine looked at Lou, still eating her breakfast. "Can I?"

Lou shrugged. "Fine by me, if Lena really doesn't mind."

Lena patted Undine's face. "I don't mind. Go and get ready—we leave in about half an hour, okay?"

Undine brushed her hair in front of the mirror in her room. She peered at herself critically. Since she had overheard Lou and Prospero fighting, and then released a flick of magic on the hillside, she had found herself avoiding Lou. It was hardly even conscious. Was she worried that Lou might see the magic in her, glittering at the corners of her eyes, resonating from her skin like gold dust? She sighed, put the brush down, and then tousled her now neat hair to fall the way she liked it.

"I've never understood why you do that," Lou said, standing in the open doorway.

Undine jumped. "Do what?" she asked guiltily.

"Brush your hair and then mess it up again. It's so . . ."

"Adolescent?" Undine offered, relieved.

"Exactly."

Undine shrugged. "One of the many mysteries that is me, I suppose."

"I didn't see much of you yesterday. I was just wondering . . ."

"You're checking up on me."

"No," Lou protested. "I just wanted to see if you're having a good time."

"Yeah, right."

"What did you get up to yesterday?"

"You *are* checking up on me!"

Lou studied Undine's face. "I'm just interested, that's all. Or is there something else you want to tell me? Should I be checking up on you?"

"No!" Did Lou know about the magic, had she felt the air tremble when that girl of butterflies, of stone and clay, had formed and unformed in front of Undine's eyes? Undine didn't think so. Perhaps Lou's successful containment of the magic for so long had made her insensitive, even from that relatively close proximity. Or perhaps Undine's magic was becoming less a confusion in the air around her and more . . . deliberate, secretive, belonging just to her. Even Prospero hadn't mentioned it, hadn't seemed to be aware that Undine had released the magic once more into the world around her.

Lou was still peering at her, so Undine said, by means of deflection, "I heard you and Prospero arguing yesterday." And then Undine realized what had been bothering her so much about what she had heard. "You said," she burst out, "that we would explore the magic together. When I've finished school. But you told Prospero yesterday I had to suppress it, that there was no place for it in my life." Lou flinched. "Well, which is it? Were you lying when you said you'd help me?"

"Not lying, not exactly. I hoped you would see . . . Oh, Undine, there's university next year. You need to focus. And then a career. Maybe a husband and children. Travel. Who knows? But do you really think you can have both? An ordinary life and the magic?"

"But it's for *me* to choose, not you." Undine felt betrayed, manipulated by Lou's promise when Lou had no intention of helping her to use the magic safely.

"We need to talk about this," said Lou, but it was a plea, not a demand. "Don't go out today."

Undine looked into Lou's eyes and realized that Lou had nothing to teach her anyway. Lou's magic was weak and dull compared to the magic that glittered inside Undine. And suddenly Undine's sense of betrayal slipped away, and she felt nothing—no anger, no remorse, perhaps a little pity, for she knew that Lou really did want what was best for her daughter.

Undine hesitated, then she swung her bag over her shoulder. "Later," she said, and set out into the courtyard to look for Lena. Lou did not follow.

The market in Corfu Town was crowded and chaotic. Glistening black and green and purple olives of different sizes were piled on tables. Huge slabs of feta and other cheeses sat in brine. Silver and gray sardines crisscrossed each other in huge metal trays without refrigeration, their surprised eyes staring mournfully at Undine. Lena stopped and talked to every stallholder in rapid Greek. Sometimes she introduced Undine and they smiled widely and greeted her: *yiasas* or *kalimera*. Undine quickly learned to say it back. Lena taught her a few more Greek phrases. Thank you was *efharisto*. *Poso kani?* How much is it?

In the friendly jostling of the markets, Undine

found it easy to forget her conversation with Lou. She absorbed her immediate environment, filling her senses so that there was no room left for Lou, or her promise, *or* the magic.

After Lena had bought enough produce to feed a smallish army, she looked at Undine thoughtfully. Lena looked at her watch; it was still early.

"I've got other errands to run. Do you want to meet me back here in a couple of hours? Will you be okay by yourself?"

Undine nodded.

Corfu Town was dusty and hot. Undine walked from the new part of the town to the old. The interior was a cluster of stone steps through the lanes, tight and compacted, and she began to feel claustrophobic in the moist, thick heat. Then she seemed to pop out the other side and found herself facing the sea. It was the harbor where the ferries from the mainland docked. Built on a piece of land jutting out to sea was the old fortress, like a fairy tale castle, grim and gray against the white-hot sky.

She followed the harbor around, thirsty and blinded by the heat. She bought a bottle of water, handing out her handful of foreign coins for the stern-faced shopkeeper to count.

"*Efharisto*," she said.

The shopkeeper smiled. "Hot?" he asked her, pointing outside his shop at the day.

"Yes."

"You walk?" He pushed a map across the counter to her. "You walk up road about two hundred meters, yes? And come to cemetery. Very nice place. Good in heat. Nice trees. You like very much."

"*Efharisto*," Undine said again. And then, gratefully, "*Thank* you."

The shopkeeper smiled quickly and nodded abruptly three times, gesticulating to her to keep the map.

Though she had her doubts about a cemetery, Undine saw immediately the shopkeeper had been right. In the heat it was a true oasis, more like a park. The trees shaded the graves, and there were flowers and grass everywhere so it was lush and cool and green. A few tourists milled around, looking at the gravestones. Some of the graves were marked with elaborate statues, others with small handmade wooden crosses or even a simple unmarked stone. Undine sat and drank her water and unwrapped a package of dried figs and cheese that Lena had slipped into her backpack.

She ate slowly, breathing in the cool garden air. She wondered if Prospero's mother and father were buried here.

Near her an old, rotund man with a walking stick stood under a tree with his eyes closed, holding a bunch of white flowers. Undine found herself watching him in an absent kind of way. He opened his eyes, and they looked straight into Undine's as if he had seen her *before* they had opened.

"Look," he said. His long stick was pointing at something on the ground: a tortoise shuffling slowly through the long grass.

"I think maybe it is my wife," the man said. He

roared with laughter, and Undine laughed too, bemused but joyful, loving the day.

Undine walked back along the harbor to the point where she had exited the old town. She retraced her steps as carefully as she could, folding and unfolding her map. Nevertheless, at some point she made a wrong turn and found herself in a mazelike jumble of streets. At times she seemed to be walking through someone's garden—there would suddenly be a cluster of pot plants, or old tins of olive oil now holding geraniums or herbs, on either side of the laneway.

She sat on a step and pulled out the map again, trying to work out where she had begun to be lost. She did not see the bald man until he was almost upon her. He shouted at her in Greek. He was old, but not as aged as many of the Greek men she had seen, his face smooth as though he had never worked in the sun.

"I'm sorry," she said, standing up quickly, folding her map clumsily against its existing creases so that it tried to balloon open again in her hand. "Sorry."

He still shouted, pushing her back the way she'd come with threatening gestures, though he did not touch her.

He switched to English. "You *no* belong here."

"Sorry, I lost my way."

"I see in your skin. In your eye. I know you. You no come here." He moaned suddenly, clutching his head. "Too much. You go."

"I'm going. I just got lost, that's all," Undine placated, though her voice trembled. What did he mean, *You don't belong here*? Was he simply referring to her foreignness, to her Australianness? But it seemed more pointed, more specific—more *personal*—and something inside Undine stirred, a kind of knowledge about herself. He was talking about the magic, she was sure of it. He *recognized* it. And it was her own fault.

She had unleashed it on the hillside, she had asked

it a question: *am I the magic or am I the girl?* And now the magic appeared to be answering her.

She backed away. "See? I'm going, okay?"

"Okay! Okay!" The man flicked his arms up into the air, shooing her away. "Okay!"

A woman came out. "Shush. Shush," she told him. "Is all right," she said to Undine. "He is . . ." she tapped her head, rolling her eyes. It was an expressive gesture. Undine smiled gratefully, though her knees shook.

Retracing her steps, quelling her shaking insides, Undine managed to find her way back to Lena, who hugged her tightly. "I thought I was going to have to tell your mother I lost you."

Undine wanted to melt into Lena's maternal arms, but something in her made her stand rigid and lonely, unyielding to Lena's hug.

Chapter Twenty-Two

In a world with little certainty, one thing was for sure: it was going to suck to be Dan when he woke up the next morning, looked out his window, and saw a blank gaping space where the Datsun should be.

The Datsun's steering was a bit on the sluggish side and the brake felt spongy under his foot. But then what would Trout know? He'd never driven a car before.

Nevertheless, he was finding he had something of a talent for it. He *loved* it. Why hadn't he done it before? By state law, at seventeen he was eligible for a provisional licence, but he'd just never got around to it. Living so close to the city, he could walk most places he wanted to go. Or there were buses, or his parents to drive him, or Dan.

But driving, he realized, wasn't about the destination. It wasn't just a more convenient way to get from A to B. It wasn't about autonomy or even freedom. It was this, the engine throbbing through him, his hands resting on the steering wheel, intuitive and responsive. It was *listening* to the car, kindly easing the gears up and down as required. It was symbiosis—the perfect fusion of mechanic and organic. It was a small internal world, a world within a world, and he controlled it. It was . . . it was *power*. It was fantastic.

"Don't you think we should slow down a little?"

Trout jumped. He had rather forgotten that the perfect fusion of mechanic and organic had a passenger. He looked at the speed dial and registered with surprise that he was a good forty kilometers over the highway's speed limit.

"Oops."

Max looked at him ironically, almost indulgently,

her left arm resting easily on the open window frame. "My mother warned me about boys like you."

"Nobody's mother warns their daughters about boys like me."

"Are you kidding?" Max ticked off on her fingers. "Bar fights. Wandering the streets at night. Meeting up with strange women from the Internet. Taking drugs. In love with some kind of powerful super-witch. Stealing cars. Driving without a license over the speed limit. Should I go on? I'm seriously running out of fingers here."

It amazed Trout to listen to Max's account of who he had become. Last year he had been an outstanding student, in love with the girl next door, dabbling in astronomy, reading Dickens and Homer and Shakespeare. He even read his science textbooks like novels, from beginning to end. Mothers loved him. He was just the kind of boy they would have wanted their daughters to bring home. But now . . .

"Trout!" Max said sharply, though she didn't look in the least concerned.

He eased his foot off the accelerator and dabbed the brake. "Sorry."

He looked sideways at Max, who had turned to stare out the window, watching the nightscape flicker past. His plan to borrow—steal, he reminded himself roughly—Dan's car and drive to the bay had not actually included Max in his mind. But when night fell, Max was still there, and having kissed her, Trout found he had neither the heart nor the complex social skills to send her home. Besides, he recognized the raw hole inside her that she hoped the magic would fill—because it mirrored his own. Perhaps by bringing her with him to the bay, he could somehow satisfy both their needs, mend both their injuries. Though, it occurred to him briefly, he hadn't actually trusted her enough to tell her where they were going or why.

They reached the hamlet of Dunalley, the occasional house radiating warm yellow light into the brittle night air. Trout slowed down considerably; it felt like they were crawling through the small town.

Suddenly Trout felt very conspicuous in the small white car lit up by the town's streetlights. He was relieved to leave the houses behind him.

"So when were you in Berlin?"

"What?"

"You said you hung out with some hackers in Berlin. Is that where you live? I mean, before you came to Tasmania?"

Max shrugged. "I've been traveling since I finished Year Twelve."

"No university? But you're so . . ."

"Smart? Thanks." Max winked. "No university; I'm a student of chaos. I'm conducting my own research."

"What kind of research?"

"I'm developing a model of the universe—based on the principles of chaos, of course."

"Really? A model of the universe? Ambitious."

"Well, it's not so much 'uni-,' as in a single uni-verse. It is and it isn't."

"A multiverse?"

"Kind of. Not quite. More . . . many in one. It's kind of layered. Dense."

"Layered? Do you mean alternative universes?"

"Exactly. But not . . . What picture do you get when you think of alternative universes?"

Trout thought. "I guess . . . a house with lots of rooms. Or, infinite earths, side by side, maybe overlapping. Flowering outward."

"Sort of . . . orderly, right? Neat?"

Trout shrugged. "I suppose so."

Max leaned forward in her seat. "In my universe, the seams are more like the continental plates: shifting, colliding, stretching thin like mozzarella cheese on a pizza, like the earth's crust."

"Colliding?"

"Yes, violently. And they're not exactly alternative, because they're pressed in against each other, they kind of coexist, crushed together. . . ."

"So the universe is folded in on itself? Like the strata of the earth's surface? Like a . . ." Trout struggled for an analogy. "Like instead of rooms in a house, maybe it's the different floors of a several-story building, and they're all caved in and squashed up. So you go through a door in the second story and suddenly you're in the third story, and something that happens on the fifth story, if it's big enough . . ."

"Can affect the first story. Yeah, sort of."

"And that's where chaos fits in?"

"Chaos is the energy that binds it all together, like . . ."

Trout knew what she was going to say. "Like the ocean. How it separates the continents . . ."

"But joins them, too. Yes!"

They grinned at each other, Trout meeting the intensity of Max's gaze briefly, until his eyes slid away, back to the road.

"So are you saying . . . ?" Trout turned it over in his mind. "Are you saying that chaos is physical? Is it an energy of some kind? Is it *matter*?"

Max slumped backward. "I think the magic is the key."

"Do you think Undine's magic is a physical manifestation of chaos?"

"I don't know. But I don't think a . . . a *sneeze* in the fifth story is going to rock the first story, if you know what I mean. I think it's just . . . immense power that would have that kind of impact."

"So why does Undine, *how* does Undine . . . ?"

"Why is she magic and not me? Or you?" Max shrugged. "I don't know. But somehow she's a conduit or . . . a physical expression of the magic. By studying her, and the events she's triggered, I hope to find out a lot more."

Trout shifted uncomfortably. To Max, Undine was a specimen, a phenomenon, something to be studied and analyzed. There were times when Trout had felt the same way, though his feelings for Undine were a constant reminder that Undine was a human girl, not a science experiment.

"So is it," Trout faltered, trying to find a way to express himself. "Is it an *atheistic* universe?"

"Are you asking me if there is a God?"

She conveyed to Trout that the question was somehow a foolish one, that it betrayed underneath his bad-ass, mother-repelling exterior his true naïveté. But he struggled to explain. "I need to know . . . if the magic . . . if it's meant to be here. *Why* Undine has it."

Max snorted. "You want to know if it was a gift from God?"

"I . . ." Trout wasn't sure what to say. He had never felt any need to believe in God before. Or to disbelieve. As a scientist, he had stayed away from the whole question of God. He didn't like the idea of attempting to prove or disprove something so unobservable, unknowable.

Something caught his attention: a patch of unremarkable highway, with a grassy verge beside it and the swinging branches of an overhanging peppermint gum. He recognized it, though it was like recognizing something from a dream. It was the patch of road to which the magic had delivered him from the bay, like a clumsily wrapped and badly addressed express-post parcel, after he had almost drowned last year.

Max screamed.

Trout's eyes snapped back to the road ahead, which was no longer ahead of them. The car was veering dangerously to the right. He wrenched the steering wheel too far to the left and the tires skidded across the road. For a moment time and space went wonky. A tree was hurtling toward them at 140 kilometers an hour, though the car itself moved in slow motion. Trout watched the scene unfold with interest, until he remembered he was not a passenger—he was in control. He wrenched the steering wheel again, and the tree was no longer in front of them. The car spun, the night whirled past. The car was filled with noise: of screeching wheels and the strangled, struggling whine of the engine and Max's screaming, though Trout didn't notice any of it until the car stopped and the engine stalled and everything, everyone, was suddenly silent.

Miraculously, they stopped on the correct side of

the road, facing the direction in which they had been driving.

Max said nothing; she stared straight ahead, her face set hard and fierce as if she was daring the road to hit her in the mouth. Her chest was heaving up and down with fear, or exhilaration, or maybe both at once. He saw in her suddenly the solitary girl he had witnessed in secret all those weeks ago, and remembered that inside the fiercely independent girl who took so many risks with her own life was another Max, one who was fragile, vulnerable, scared of a group of silly girls.

It took his breath—it was like it was the first time he really recognized her. Suddenly it seemed less astonishing, less of a coincidence that they should be together and more to do with design, a pattern that had been laid out for them. And right now it didn't feel like a cosmic joke. It felt . . . comforting.

Their eyes met, and Max stared at him for a moment like an animal caught in the headlights, dazed, dazzled, by their shared encounter with death.

Trout knew he mirrored her expression. Then suddenly they were laughing: hysterical, relieved, adrenaline-filled laughter. The coarse sound tore at the rarefied air around them. It was a kind of wild, senseless laughing, and Trout loved it. It felt like living.

And then they were silent again, apart from the occasional gasp of leftover laughter. They smiled softly at each other, as the cool night air blew in through Max's open window and across her skin to rest lightly on Trout's, carrying with it her sweet and sour citrusy faint fragrance. Max's face was lit by moonlight and Trout was struck once again by how beautiful her features were—somehow the moonlight on her pale skin made her seem at once more fragile and more resilient.

With surprisingly steady hands, Trout turned the key and fired the engine. His foot was firm but gentle on the accelerator as he drove the short distance to the turnoff to the bay.

CHAPTER TWENTY-THREE

"Wanna come for a walk?" Sofia leaned in the open doorway of Undine's hotel room. "Mum's driving me mental."

"Are you kidding? Your mum's great!" Undine's fingers were sticky from a huge slab of Lena's homemade baklava. "Swap you."

"As long as I get a cute baby brother with the bargain."

"Sold."

They headed toward the village, both of them scuffing their shoes along the loose, gravelly road. Their conversation was as winding and aimless as their walking. Sofia told Undine about her travel plans; Undine told Sofia—halfheartedly—about Dominic, who she realized was still officially her boyfriend, though Undine had not thought about him at all until Sofia asked.

"He sounds cute."

Undine shrugged. "He is . . . I guess."

"Like that, is it? So why are you going out with him?"

"I don't know." And Undine realized she really didn't know. Yes, he was there and convenient, and it seemed like she should have a boyfriend . . . but he was a person, too. He deserved a girlfriend who cared about—who even noticed—his finer qualities. "I think we're going to break up. When I get home."

Sofia nodded. They drifted for a few more minutes in silence.

"You're in your last year of school, right?" Sofia asked eventually.

"Yep."

"So what are your plans for next year?"

Undine always dreaded this question. Trout had any number of useful and fulfilling career paths ahead of him and rattled them off at alarming speed. Fran always laughed, declaring herself to be finished with school, though she didn't lack ambition. Undine guessed Fran would end up working for her father in his real estate business—or rather, that Fran's father would end up working for Fran. Even Dominic had known he wanted to be an architect since he was eleven years old. But for Undine the question immediately reminded her that her only vision of the future was of a ragged gaping black hole.

What could she *be*? What would the magic let her be? A florist, a baker, a teacher, a brain surgeon? These were all someone else's futures, not Undine's.

"I don't know," Undine mumbled, embarrassed. "I haven't really thought about it." She felt like a child and that Sofia, who had finished an economics degree, was the grown-up.

Sofia sensed Undine's discomfort. "Plenty of time to decide," she said.

"Yeah," said Undine, but for the second time that

day she had the peculiar sensation that time was rushing past, whistling by her ears, leaving her behind. The magic was outside time. It was ageless, or perhaps just very, very ancient: a human life was a mere blink to the magic, even Undine's life.

Sofia was still looking at her. "You're not upset about what that man said today, are you?"

"How did you know about that?"

"I overheard my mum telling yours."

"Oh."

"They reckon it's to do with magic," Sofia said casually, but she watched Undine for her response.

Undine was astounded. "*You* know about the magic?"

"Oh, yeah. It's a bit of a family myth. I don't believe in it, though," she added quickly, her jaw hard with stubbornness. Suddenly, in a swift reversal, Sofia was the mulish child and Undine was old—older than anyone had ever been.

Undine laughed.

"What's so funny?" Sofia asked.

"Oh. Nothing. Tell me the myth, then."

"Something to do with some woman, deep in the family's past. It's actually like the real fairy tale, you know: a fisherman falls in love with a mermaid, so he hides her fish suit or sealskin or whatever so she'll stay. And she loves him back and has babies with him, but she's always staring longingly out to sea. Then one day their oldest child asks why their father keeps an old sealskin coat hidden in the house's rafters, and the woman finds it and leaves her kids and husband and goes back to the sea. Do you know it?"

"Versions of it. Not about our family, though. Just in books."

"The family story isn't quite the same. Just that a woman washed up on shore—probably jumped off a slaver's ship or something—and married a local and had babies, and then one day she swam out to sea and never returned. She probably just drowned. You know how stories get all twisted up by time."

"And she was magic?"

"That was how the story went, that this woman

brought some kind of magic with her. And then her children, and her children's children and so on, all had a bit of this magic. Mum used to tell me when I was a kid, but when I realized she really believed in it, I was embarrassed and made her stop telling me. You know, like I ate Vegemite sandwiches and wagged Saturday morning Greek school to play netball, and made everyone call me Sophie. I didn't want my wog mum telling me her wog stories. I don't feel like that anymore, of course," she added, "but magic? Come on. You don't really believe in that stuff, do you?"

For the briefest of moments, Undine itched to show Sofia what she could do, to prove to her that she was more than an aimless, ambitionless child. The magic wanted to show off. Conjure up a storm or a girl, change a tree into a frog, or make snow fall from the clear blue sky.

But she did none of those things. She held the magic in, kept it safe and secret under her skin.

• • •

Grunt had not seemed surprised to see Trout pull up outside Prospero's house close to midnight, though that was possibly because surprise was too *exuberant* an emotion for Grunt. Not that Grunt lacked emotion; he was just . . . uncomplicated. He took things as they came, and Trout respected him for it.

Together Grunt and Trout made up two beds while Max hung back—shyly, Trout supposed.

"Different rooms?" Grunt asked, his arms full of blankets.

"What? *Oh.*" Trout blushed. "Yes, please."

Richard would have winked or made a bawdy joke; Dan's voice would have been disapproving, even faintly loathing. But Grunt managed to ask it in the same voice he used minutes later to ask Trout how many sugars he took in his coffee, and Trout was grateful for it.

He found Max on the veranda. "Coffee?" he asked her. "Grunt's making some."

"Don't you *ever* sleep?" she asked. "I'm exhausted."

Trout blinked in surprise. "Um. Didn't we sleep this morning?"

"Some people," Max said, as if she was revealing a great secret, "sleep *every* night. Eight hours. More, even. You should try it."

Trout looked at Max, again remembering the nights he had seen her, weeks before, when she hadn't been sleeping. He remembered especially the night she had sat up in her flat, unable to sleep, glancing at the door where the brick had been thrown. Of course he didn't mention it, but he couldn't keep the tone of sympathy out of his voice as he joked, "Eight hours? Really? And you recommend it?"

Max glanced at him curiously, but went along with his banter. "Good for the soul."

"The soul? I thought you didn't believe in God?"

Max's voice took on an American evangelist twang. "I *believe* in sleep."

"Sleep's for wusses."

"That's another finger."

"What?"

"Another reason my mum wouldn't like you. Early

to bed, early to rise." Max yawned as if to make her point. "Take me to bed or lose me forever."

Trout blanched.

"Joke," Max said. "Except I do really need to go to bed."

Trout showed her to the room farthest from the front door, where a fold-out bed sat in the middle of a sea of boxes and other junk.

"Sorry about the mess," Trout said, though he could hardly be blamed for it.

"Polite, though. That's one finger in your favor."

"Just one? Tell her I came third in the national math competition last year. Mothers like that sort of thing, don't they?"

"Third? I'm impressed."

Max seemed to hover beside Trout as if she expected something. He looked at the rounded, luscious shape of her mouth.

"Good night," she murmured.

"Good night," Trout said, and shut the door on those lips. They reminded him why he was here. If he *could* reclaim his life, perhaps he could legitimately claim those lips, too.

Third in the national math competition, and yet still the most profoundly stupid boy Max had ever met. So why did it bother her so much that he didn't want to kiss her?

Suddenly Max missed Europe. She missed its cities—cities of chaos: Madrid, Berlin, Amsterdam, London, Athens. They stayed up all night dancing; they wielded weather with celestial humor, weather that spun you around; they were cobbled and cluttered and crowded. She knew where she was in a city. She could look in a map, read a guidebook, and learn which streets to avoid after dark, where the crazies and the druggies and the desperates hung out. But here, on this island, the hazards were hidden; there was no map. She didn't know which streets, which mountains, which other beautiful, gilded landscapes to avoid. All of them were treacherous. Yes, she knew where she was in a city. There was no Mount Wellington hovering at the periphery, watching your every move with the mild reproval of a remote parent; no mountain which could just as easily gobble you, digest you, and leave only the bones of you. There was no . . . *this* place, mysterious, secretive, entirely unavailable to her. There was no . . .

There was no Trout.

And now she didn't know which places to avoid *within* her, because she could be traveling along quite nicely, and all of a sudden she would turn a corner or cross a road and there she would be, moving with a dangerous velocity toward him. Not Trout, her father. His image was everywhere; his face was scorched into the mountain's rugged side. He was everywhere, but he was nowhere—every street corner she turned she wanted to find him, she expected it, that he would be magicked out of the island's very air. But she found nothing. Nothing but those beautiful gilded boys, all shining and earnest and resonating with love. Like that other one, Charlie, the one she had almost managed to forget. But the love wasn't for her, was it? Not his, nor Trout's. Always instead for some island girl, shimmering with gold on the outside but silver as ice within.

CHAPTER TWENTY-FOUR

That evening, when Jasper and Lou were taking a swim in the last of the day's light, Undine said to her father, "He was right, wasn't he?"

Prospero drifted and drowsed.

"What?" he asked, thick with sleep. "Who?"

"Last year, when I was in the sea, I became more the magic and less the girl, less human. I *don't* belong here. I don't mean Corfu, I mean . . ." and Undine gestured expansively around her. "I'm from—parts of me—are from somewhere else. Somewhere . . . remote."

The old man leaned forward and held out his frail hand, searching the air for hers. "Listen to me," Prospero said when her hand found his, his voice strong. "Before I knew you, I thought you were special for your magic. I thought that was what I wanted. It's powerful and impressive and it's intoxicating. But I see you now, who you are. The magic is part of you, but it's not the most impressive, the most powerful part of you. That's the girl, my daughter. And I missed so many years.

"You *do* belong here. You belong *here* in this landscape because you come from me, and I came from my mother who came from this land. You belong *here*, next to me because I am your father and I love you. You belong here," and Prospero thumped his chest. "And you belong here," he gestured vaguely at the hotel, "with your mother and your brother. And with Lena and Sofia."

The girl inside Undine who wanted a father and a family was moved by the tenderness of Prospero's words. She wanted to tell him about the girl she had created made of stone and butterflies and packed earth. She wanted to explain to him about the magic, how she could feel it here in Greece in the same way she had felt it in the bay, taking her over.

But she couldn't—she felt the space that existed between herself and her father, between herself and everyone, everything, balloon. Once upon a time, she had thought her father could teach her about the magic within her, but how could he? This pale, fading man . . . he had once wanted the magic himself, wanted to possess it. But he was nothing compared to her; he was a shadow, an echo, reflecting back her own power; he was a mere child playing at his mother's skirt.

"I'm going to bed," she said, and she leaned over Prospero where he sat and kissed his leathery cheek. He closed his eyes at her kiss and she felt tenderness and compassion wash over her. She lingered for a moment. Time was unmaking him, she observed; old age was grinding him away, piece by piece. But, she was beginning to realize, time was not for her. Time, space, this land, this sea, even Prospero and Jasper and Lou—all of them belonged to a place remote and foreign to Undine.

On her way to her room, Undine saw Lou's door was open. Jasper was alone, sleeping right in the center of the double bed, his fist curled up in his moist and springy blond curls. Undine went in and sat on the bed beside him. She swept his hair off his face. Jasper slept on.

"Hi." Lou stepped out of the bathroom wearing Chinese silk pajamas; her damp blond hair sprang up in curls around her face, like Jasper's. She smelled of the sea.

"Hi," Undine echoed, softly.

Lou smiled down at Jasper. "I remember watching you sleep like that. I could have let off an explosion right by your head and you wouldn't have stirred." She sat on the bed next to Undine. "About this morning, the things we said . . ."

Undine shook her head. "It doesn't matter. I have to find my own path. You understand that, don't you?"

"I just don't want you to make the mistakes I did."

"What mistakes?"

Lou sighed. "I didn't want to tell you about this yet. I wanted to wait."

"Prospero said, what's left to grow in the dark, neglected, grows up wrong, and I think he's right. At least for me."

Lou said, "You're young. You think you know . . . but you don't."

"Then tell me. *Tell* me."

"When I met Prospero, my parents made me choose—him or them." She smiled unhappily at Undine. "I know you must think it's strange that I wanted Prospero. I was so young and he's so old. But I grew up in a grim house, with lots of angry whispers and sharp words. Sometimes I feel like I'm still pulling out the shrapnel of those words, digging it out from deep inside my skin, right down to the bones. Prospero was . . . Did I ever tell you how we met?" Undine shook her head. "He was my first-year university lecturer."

"Really?" Undine couldn't imagine it—Prospero seemed so disconnected from the world. She supposed it made sense that he'd had a job once: after all, he owned a house, and seemed to feed himself and pay his electricity bills and buy socks and things, so it stood to reason that he had earned money at some point in his life. "How . . . *racy.* What subject?"

"Philosophy. I loved it; all these new ideas filled me, fed me, nurtured me in a way my stifling upbringing never had. And I was such a kid and he was a grown-up and he made me feel like I was one, too. And when he started talking about the magic— and all this time I'd felt it growing inside me, terrifying and exciting and desirable and unwelcome all at once—it was like he could see straight into the heart of me." Lou tilted her head and thought for a moment. Her eyes sparkled, mischievously. "Plus he was kinda sexy for an old man."

"Lou!"

"I'm trying to be honest with you. It's what you wanted, isn't it? Anyway, I chose Prospero, and my parents basically told me I could never come back."

"But they were awful."

"They were, and I was glad to leave. And I did enjoy testing my power with Prospero—together we were both stronger than either of us was individually. Prospero had already discovered the potency of the Bay of Angels. I dropped out of uni, he quit his position: not because of our relationship—it wasn't so very uncommon in those days—but because we wanted to devote all our time to exploring our powers."

"What did you do?"

Lou shook her head. "It seemed so important at the time. So impressive. But it was all frivolous. We changed the weather, we called up fire, we made the earth roll like the sea, we transformed things—drops of water into glistening pebbles, dry, dead sticks into living trees. The only thing we did, the only thing of any meaning, was you. We made you. Not with magic, but I can't say it was love that made you either. We didn't love each other. Well, I knew by then I didn't love him; I don't know if he loved me."

Undine thought about this: she wasn't born from love. A few days ago the thought would have made her sad, but now . . . the words rolled over her and washed away into nothing.

"After you were born," Lou went on, "things changed. I wasn't interested in the magic anymore. I wanted to be a family for you, be the family I didn't have. I wanted to love you, to buy you things, to dress you prettily. I was proud of you, I wanted to show the world to you and you to the world. Most of all, I wanted you to live in the world, not hidden away in the bay. I left Prospero."

"He let you leave?"

"He begged me to stay. He was desperate. He even threatened me, but I think I knew he would never deliberately hurt me . . . or you."

"Did he love me?"

Lou frowned. "I don't know. Maybe. I don't think he could separate you from the magic. He wanted to own you; he wanted to own the magic. He wanted to own me, too, but he couldn't. Without love, he had no claim over me. And my magic was stronger than his."

"Was that when you moved into the flat in Bellerive?"

"Not straightaway. I went . . . I went back to my parents. I thought once they saw you, knew they were grandparents, that things might change." Lou smiled. "You were a *lovely* baby."

"But they didn't think so."

Lou shook her head. "When they looked at you, with such . . . such bitterness . . ." Lou closed her eyes, as if she could see her parents' expressions in front of her and couldn't bear to look at them again. "You were six months old—not even. You had a smile that would break the sky apart. And they were *cold* to you. All they could see of you was the monster inside, the magic. I promised myself then that the magic was over. That no one would look at you like that again. I thought . . . I thought I could end it. I pushed it down, and I swear, Undine, it went away. At first, it was hard. And there were times when you and I fought, especially after we lost Stephen. . . ." Lou's voice cracked. "I felt so angry, so *shattered*. I had to leave, just drive and drive, or it would . . . it threatened to bubble back up, to leak out of the cracks, and I knew if I let it out, I wouldn't be able to control it."

Undine didn't need Lou to remind her what it had been like to lose Stephen. The very mention of his name could conjure his face so clearly in her mind, she could almost touch it. Stephen and Lou had been to Undine these two enormous, radiating suns, and when one of them had been extinguished, Lou had had to become more immense to take his place. But to Undine now Lou seemed small, and as she talked she grew smaller still, until it was as if Undine could nestle her in the palm of her hand like a pearl.

"Did Stephen know? About the magic?"

"I didn't tell him. I hid it; I thought I hid it so

well. But Stephen, he loved me more closely, more attentively than anyone ever had in my life. If anyone could find it, he could, and he did. He told me . . ." Lou drifted off.

"Lou?"

"He told me it was beautiful. That I shouldn't be ashamed. And sometimes he-even got angry; he thought I should tell you, teach you. But I was sure if I kept it hidden, I could make it go away, that you wouldn't have to . . . I'm sorry. I only wanted to protect you."

From very far away, Undine said, "It's okay." She felt herself drifting again, suspended over Lou in some way rather than sitting beside her.

Undine knew she was sidestepping time, or time was sidestepping her, and that her place in this world was transient, fleeting. This story, about grandparents she did not remember who had not wanted her anyway, only served to remind Undine of the precarious place she held in the universe. Lou had been able to suppress the magic, but only barely, and Undine sensed that it had not been without some cost to Lou. Besides, Undine knew *she* was different. Holding the magic in, it would kill her eventually: she would fall apart into nothing, into stones and clay, ephemeral as butterflies.

Suddenly she felt the promise she had made to Lou—which had been a relief and a burden—fall from her like her she'd dropped a heavy stone: a stone that had weighed her down, yes, but also had prevented her from being pulled away by the strong currents. It was good to put the stone down, but it was frightening, too, for now there was nothing to hold her back.

Jasper stirred and grimaced as if dreaming. Absently, Lou stroked his back, lulling him to sleep. Undine kissed Lou as lightly as she had Prospero earlier, and to her lips Lou's face felt papery and rough.

"Good night," she said.

When Undine reached the dark space of the door Lou said, "If you use it, if you choose the magic, you might lose us, Jasper and me. You might not find your way home."

Into the shadows of the courtyard, Undine said, too softly for Lou to hear, "If I don't use it, I might lose me."

CHAPTER TWENTY-FIVE

Trout lay awake in the dark. He stared at the ceiling. He was engaged with *missing* her; it was like a chore he had neglected. When Undine had said that her feelings for him would never change, she had taken a long loose cord that bound them together and severed it. But nevertheless, it was tangled around him, wrapped around his heart tightly enough to amputate it from his body. She had merely floated away, like a balloon that had been tethered to him by his longing.

He was lying there, thinking about the life ahead of him with no heart, when the door clicked open and Max slipped into the room. Her naked body was long, lean, pale, white-brown like almonds. She said nothing, and neither did Trout, though his stomach spasmed and for a moment he thought he might vomit—he might vomit Undine straight out of his guts, leaving a space for Max.

She lay down beside him, and the single bed creaked, protesting against the added weight but rearranging its springs to accommodate her. Trout felt her body, unnaturally smooth and hard and cool to touch, as if she were part shark. Trout did not entirely command his hands; it seemed of their own accord they explored her, trying to determine her exact composition.

He didn't want her, but he did. She was sensual, desirable, but his heart wasn't in it. He didn't love her. Thinking of Undine and how abandoned he'd felt by her rejection of him, perhaps he owed it to Max to try; after all, it wasn't like he felt nothing for Max at all.

He wanted to want her, that was it. He wanted to replace Undine with Max.

Trout kissed Max and she kissed him back. His hands found the cool, smooth curve of her back.

Appallingly, he realized he didn't need his heart for this. Perhaps love was overrated. Or maybe sex was more reliable, more honest.

Max used her body like a paintbrush; it acted on him with bold, clear strokes. As the night progressed, Trout found that, without his heart, sex was not unlike death: it obliterated you, you disappeared, and all that was left was the body.

"I feel it," Max whispered, her face over his. "I feel it all the time."

Trout looked up at her. "What?" he asked, nervously.

"The magic. It trembles inside me, just out of reach."

Afterward, Max lay with her face soft and relaxed, a whisper of a smile on her lips, smelling peculiarly of sun-dried washing and orange peel.

But Trout's dying heart flopped like a fish, ticking and twitching in the cold dry night, and his lungs opened and closed, searching for air.

Trout left Max sleeping. She didn't stir as he

pulled on his jeans, a shirt, and the heavy, knobbly jumper his mother had knitted from homespun wool. In the faint moon and starlight he staggered across the garden, and found the path that split the dunes and led him to the sea.

The water was a dark black-blue, as if the earth was stained. He searched the water with his eyes, peering through the darkness. He studied it like it was a book, full of text: a decipherable system of symbols and codes. He looked in the bay for himself, for that past, old Trout who, in one way or another, had been taken by this place.

Cold penetrated him; it made his eyes ache and his body weak. But he maintained his vigil. He looked for Trout, and for Trout's heart, and for Trout's breath.

When the sun rose, he was still searching.

Max entered the kitchen wrapped in a sheet. She expected Trout, but found his friend. What was his name, something weird? Grunt?

"Morning," she said.

Grunt raised his eyebrows slightly, though not apparently embarrassed by her state of undress. "Morning."

Max helped herself to the muesli on the bench. "Where's Trout?"

"Haven't seen him. I assume he's not up yet."

Max said nothing.

Grunt looked at her circumspectly. She found the silence in the kitchen unnerving. She tilted her head. He was good-looking, sexier than Trout with his surfer's body and dreadlocked hair. He wasn't awkward like Trout. He had that inner calm thing going, like maybe he did yoga or Tai Chi or something. He met her gaze and seemed to study her, too.

She smiled. "Have we met?" Max asked through a mouthful of muesli. "You seem familiar."

Grunt continued to examine her before saying, "I'm a friend of Charlie's. And Johanna's."

Max's face froze. She got up. "I have to . . . I have to get dressed."

She stood in the hallway, her heart thumping. It was stupid. It was so stupid. It was *nothing*. It was this place, this island, so cramped, things kept coming back to you. You lived your life in a glass bubble, relentlessly observed. In other places—in cities—people fell in and out of love all the time. They betrayed each other, they met someone else, they had brief, intimate interludes, and then they disappeared. The city forgave them. But Hobart was like a maiden aunt, holding a magnifying glass to every ill affair of the human heart. Hobart gossiped and bitched; Hobart was haughty and sanctimonious.

Max went back to her room, dressed, and sat on the bed running her hands through her hair. What was happening to her? What progress was she making? She wasn't here for Trout, she told herself savagely. She hadn't flown halfway across the world with the money she inherited from her father to fall in love. She was here for the magic. She was here to reclaim what had been taken from her, and the magic was the only way she could do that.

She could smell Trout on her skin, but suddenly Undine hung like a specter around her—or was it just Grunt reminding her of Johanna? She remembered the bang of the brick hitting her front door like a small explosion, the feeling of its rough texture when she'd cradled it in the palm of her hand as she'd retreated inside. No. No. She pushed Johanna away. It was Undine. But not . . . There was something, but she couldn't quite catch it in her mind, like a half-remembered song. She thought back to the kitchen, her bowl of muesli, getting the milk out of the fridge. That was it! A photo on the fridge—Undine. She'd been here. The magic. It was something to do with this place. That's why Trout had brought her here, even though he hadn't wanted to tell her why. After all, he was searching for it, too.

Charlie and Johanna forgotten, Max thought about Undine and smiled. She got up from the bed, buoyant with the possibilities of what she might discover, and went looking for Trout.

• • •

Grunt found him first. Trout sat on the beach, his arms tucked inside his jumper for warmth. His eyes were fixed on the farthest of the stone "angels" that the bay was named for.

"Great place to watch the sun rise," said Grunt.

"Is it?" Trout blinked at the sky, realizing that it had lightened to blue. "Oh, yes."

Grunt sat next to him on the sand.

"You know," Grunt said, and stopped, as if reconsidering what he'd been about to say. He tilted his head to one side as if the right words might slide into place. Then he ploughed on, "There's something out there, under the sea."

"Yeah?" Trout asked, numb from lack of sleep.

"It . . ." Grunt hesitated and then said, almost apologetically, "It glows."

"Glows?"

"Kind of pulses." Grunt shook his head, having trouble describing it. The more words he tried to pin to it, the more it resisted any kind of language at all. "It's like . . . liquid light . . . energy . . . electrons spinning . . . like . . ."

But Trout knew. "Like Undine," he said flatly.

"Like Undine."

"Can you show me?"

Grunt studied him. Trout continued to stare out to sea, his face unchanged, but Grunt could almost see the hunger and emptiness gnawing in Trout. "You ever dived?" Grunt asked.

Trout shook his head.

"I do have spare equipment," Grunt admitted. "All the uni stuff is in the boat shed. But I don't know. It's not an easy dive for a beginner. Visibility's not great."

"But you could guide me. Couldn't you? And if there's any trouble . . . if I can't handle it, we could just come back up."

"But if we *both* got into trouble . . . If we got separated . . ."

Trout thought about it, alone in the darkness of

the bay, under its surface in its internal world. Trout wasn't afraid. Just him, facing it. This was right, it *fit*. This was what he needed to do. And if the bay took him, then . . . that was what was meant to be. He almost hoped it would.

He set his jaw. "I'm not afraid of being alone."

He saw Max standing at the peak of the dunes looking down at them.

"I'll do it with your help," Trout said urgently, "or I'll do it without you. I can get a wet suit, equipment. I can come back on my own. . . ."

"You could," said Grunt, unmoved. "I couldn't stop you. It doesn't mean I should help you. You could die down there."

"Please," Trout begged. "You know. Of everyone, everyone in the world, you *know* . . . you know her. You know *me*. You know the magic. Grunt, I need you. I need your help. I have to do this. . . ." Trout could hear his urgency breaking in his voice.

Grunt looked out to sea. He shook his head, as if

arguing with himself. "If I help—*if*—you have to stay close. You have to come up if I tell you to. First sign of trouble . . ."

"I promise. Thank you."

"Yeah, well. Rule number one. Don't die."

Trout smiled, but the smile was insubstantial as the thin winter sky.

He and Grunt watched as Max headed down from the peak of the dunes toward them.

"What's going on with you and her?" Grunt asked curiously, while Max was still out of earshot.

"What do you mean?"

"Do you trust her?"

"Yes!" Trout said defensively, then hesitated. "I mean . . . why? Do you know her?"

"Not really. Sort of. She hangs out with a weird crowd. Kind of unpleasant. That girl, the one who gave you drugs at Duncan's party. She's one of them."

Trout looked hard at Grunt. "They're friends?"

Grunt nodded.

Trout suddenly remembered what Max had said in the car about boys like him. She had known about the drugs, but how? Trout hadn't told her. Damn it! How could he have been so blind? So stupid? How could he have ever trusted her?

"What's going on?" said Max as she approached.

"I'll go and . . . do stuff," said Grunt, his mistrust of Max clear.

Max sat down next to Trout. He didn't look at her.

"How are you this morning?" Max asked softly. "You disappeared. I woke up and you were gone."

"You didn't tell me you knew Eliza," Trout said, his voice quiet and flat.

Max shook her head. "I—"

"Just don't," Trout said. "Don't *lie*. I don't want to hear it." And he sat staring out at the sea.

Max sat beside him, waiting.

"Trout, I—"

Trout turned to her. "You arranged it. All of it. The drugs. The beating at the pub. It was all you, trying to *get* to me. There was never anyone following us. Was there?" He laughed, bitterly. "All that stuff about the Chaosphere and a virus—it was all rubbish, wasn't it? You probably planted the virus yourself, before you let me into the house. I can't believe you played me . . . and I let myself . . . God! You must think I'm so easy. What a walkover. Is that what last night was about to you, too? Getting to me, getting into my head? You disgust me."

Max stared out to sea, struck dumb. She didn't try to deny what Trout was saying. She sat there, her muteness an admission of her guilt.

Trout stood up. "You should go," he said bitterly. "Walk up to the road, hitch a ride. I don't want to see you anymore."

Finally, Max said, "I'm not the only one, am I?"

"What?"

Max's voice was hard and splintery. "Keeping secrets. Following. You came to my flat. You were there, the night Johanna and her stupid cronies threw that brick at my door, painted on my driveway. You watched it happen."

"You saw me?" Trout's voice faltered; his moral stance had been so unfailing a moment before, but now he didn't know.

Max's eyes were slanted with anger. "I didn't know it was you then, but I saw you."

"But . . . I didn't know you. It was just . . . I was just there. . . ."

"It's not so clear, is it? Nothing's so clear as you think."

Trout remembered the other night, when he had peered in at her through the crack in her curtains. He felt suddenly, hotly, how wrong that had been. Did she know about that night, too?

"And that night at the pub. You thought *you* were following *me*." Max laughed dryly.

"Because that's what you wanted me to think!"

"Who's to blame? You came into the pub of your own accord. You wanted to; you wanted *me*. You wanted me to obliterate *her*, to wipe her out of your mind."

"I didn't want to be beaten up by a couple of thugs."

"Didn't you? Are you sure? Or is that exactly what you were looking for all those nights you walked the streets? Someone to do for you what you were too weak, too gutless, to do yourself?"

"I don't have to listen to this." Trout turned in disgust—shared equally between himself and Max—and walked away.

Undine dreams about Trout.

They sit together on a stone wall at school, overlooking the gray river.

"The magic," she remarks. "It isn't to *do* things, you know."

"I know."

"That's just a side effect."

Trout nods. They sit in silence.

Trout says, "I'm descending."

Undine squeezes his hand. "I know you are."

Trout looks at Undine, peers right inside her. "Who's going to die for you?" he asks.

She looks up at the blue sky and realizes it's suddenly summer. Birds wheel overhead, tumbling joyfully through the sky. The grass glistens green and bright, the yellow flowers are dizzy as suns.

But next to her Trout is gray; winter hangs around him like a drab gray coat. Undine leans in, whispers into him, "Never mind. It's almost spring."

CHAPTER TWENTY-SIX

Max watched the boys haul the boat along the sand and into the water.

At first when Trout had walked up the beach, she thought he was merely escaping her. But Trout had met Grunt at the end of the beach, and they'd gone into the weathered wooden boathouse in the crest of the dunes, emerging dressed in wet suits and carrying an oxygen tank. What were they up to? Grunt was obviously boaty; she recognized the type, with his sun-bleached dreads and his salt-dry skin. But Trout? She hadn't seen it in him at all—he was baby soft and *protected*, as if he had suffered from a childhood illness or overmothering or both, as if someone had told him he couldn't run like the other boys.

Even from her distant lookout, she could tell he'd never pushed a boat into the water. His body was all overlong, clumsy limbs as he struggled to climb into it once it was seaborne. She felt a rush of affection but was simultaneously annoyed by his weakness, his softness.

She watched their progress as she walked up the beach to the shed. The billowing sail dropped when they reached the furthest of the stone formations that jutted out of the water, a few kilometers from shore.

She turned her attention to the boat shed. The padlock swung open on the unbolted lock. She almost laughed. They were so trusting. Well, that wasn't really true. Trout had trusted her, or had started to, but not anymore. Grunt didn't trust her either, but he underestimated her; he believed the only real threat she posed was to Trout's heart. She felt tears threatening to sting her eyes, and she pinched herself hard on her arm to make it stop. She would not allow herself to care about Trout, to care about his heart—his damaged, pitiable heart. It was not for her anyway, despite last night.

Her eyes adjusted to the shed's dim light. There was another boat in there, a small aluminum one with an outboard motor. There was more equipment, too. She held a wet suit up to herself for size. She cleared the mess from around the small boat and dragged it to the open door, piling the diving gear inside.

On the beach, she wriggled out of her clothes—Undine's clothes—feeling a fleeting thrill as the cold air hit her naked body. She loved the feel of a wet suit, the sleek rubber casing sliding onto her like a second skin. She had spent whole summers underwater, diving with her father, looking upward at distant fractured surfaces of oceans, or sideways into the glittering eyes of astonished fish. The black rubber suit was like a shark skin, which suited her. She was a shark herself—she had to keep moving to breathe and stay afloat.

From the raised vantage point of the boat shed door, she watched as first one, then the other distant figure dropped over the side of their sailboat into the bay, and then she hauled the aluminum boat up the beach, past the tide line, and into the sea.

Trout floated down alongside the bowline gradually, with Grunt behind him. He followed Grunt's instructions—holding his nose and breathing out through it to maintain his equilibrium. He felt urine trickle out and the layer of water between the wet suit and his bare skin warmed up; the warmth cocooned him. He breathed the tank's oxygen, and it sounded noisy in his own ears. He kept his breaths regular, not too shallow but avoiding the urge to hyperventilate.

He looked up. He could see the keel of the boat under the water and beyond it the surface, and suddenly he was hit by an intense surge of claustrophobia, as if the sea's lid had closed him in. He swallowed air. He fought the urge to kick his way back to the surface and continued down the line.

He didn't look up again. Instead, he switched on his torch and looked around him. Kelp dragged itself to and fro like the matted hair of washerwomen beating cloth on rocks. Intermittent fish darted in and out of his peripheral vision. He descended, into the seaweed forest. He kept his breathing regular and his body calm as he entered the thick swathes of it, though his urge to panic, to fight the seaweed away, was strong.

He held the bowline like a thick, knotted umbilical, holding him to the mother—earth, land, sky. He stopped climbing down and looked around him. The kelp swayed; Trout swayed. Was he an interloper? Did he belong here? Had the bay been waiting for him? If he let go, would the sea be quick to claim him, to turn him into a sea thing, or would it reject him, toss him—spent and broken—onto the shore?

He closed his eyes and let go. He opened his eyes again.

Grunt turned to make sure Trout was following

and then kicked his way through the thick kelp forest. Trout kept him in his sights, leaving the anchored bowline hanging solemnly behind him. "It's easy to get disoriented down there," Grunt had warned. How would he find his way back if he lost Grunt, he wondered, as the bowline disappeared behind a sheath of kelp. At the same time he knew return was not necessarily the imperative of this journey. After all, a life for a life—wasn't his life forfeit to this sea? Would the sea take him?

He swam slowly downward, kicking his way toward the sea floor. He saw the wreck, the enormous broken ship, its hull gaping, wounded. The sea had begun to claim it; the life of the sea had taken hold of the dead vessel—things grew and scuttled and swam in places where humans once slept. Trout drifted past the wreck and found he was not interested in disturbing its secrets or raiding its treasures or listening to its groaned myths.

His eyes searched for light.

But he heard it before he saw it. It was not hearing

like it would be on the surface, in the air, his ears translating vibrations into sound. He seemed to hear it with his breastplate, in the core of him. As Grunt had said, it was the same as it had been standing next to Undine, in the eye of her magical storm.

He drew closer, the noise expanding inside him, and then his eyes made out the glow. Grunt stopped, letting Trout pass him. As Trout drew closer to the light, his fingers automatically outstretched and he did what Grunt had not been foolish enough to do. He made contact. He touched it. He touched it, and it was the magic itself he touched, as if he had wrested Undine to the ground, torn her skin open, and plunged his hand inside her, beyond viscera to the magic's very heart.

Undine woke as if she were on fire. She clutched her burning diaphragm; her bottom ribs were like hot steel knives. Something was happening at the pit of her self, in the depths of her where the magic lived.

Someone—someone other, someone outside her—was plundering her, delving inside her as if she were a cupboard and they were looking for lost belongings in her darkest depths.

(That was what the magic was, she thought, abruptly, irrelevantly—a sea of lost things—whole civilizations submerged, stars and moons and vanished children and kings, spent hearts, moth wings.)

The pain was unbearable; it tore through her as if it might rip her into pieces.

And then, as abruptly as it had started, the pain stopped, and she was alone again, her body and the magic intact, the intruder, for the time being, repelled. She gasped, swallowing night air, and felt herself become whole again.

Max steered the small motorized boat, feeling the engine throbbing her arm. Her father used to take her sailing. He would take his hands off the tiller and hold them in the air.

"Oh, my *god*!" he would cry, waggling his fingers. "No one's driving the boat. It's out of control!" And she would take over, steering their course. He trusted her, he trusted her not to steer them into troubled waters. And if she lost her way, his hand would fold over hers, guiding them both to safety.

She shook her head as if to shake him out of her mind. She'd trusted *him* and in doing so had learned she could trust no one. Who had guided him? He had steered himself into dark, mysterious waters and had left her behind, high and dry, gasping in an alien atmosphere.

Max eased the dinghy to sit alongside Grunt's sailboat. She adjusted the borrowed wet suit—it hung a little baggily around her shoulders and waist, but it would do. She checked her equipment again. She felt a momentary sweep of the exhilaration she always experienced just before a dive, then she let herself fall backward into the water and floated. She deflated the buoyancy vest, fitted the regulator into her mouth, and began to descend, ignoring the bowline, trusting to Chaos, delivering herself to the bay.

When Trout extracted his hand from the globe of light, he was dismayed to find he was still present, intact, unchanged. He hung for a moment, suspended in the black water surrounding the light; his mind felt broken and frayed.

Grunt signaled to him. Trout gazed blankly before forcing his legs to move, following Grunt through the forest of seaweed. Grunt's flippers kicked in and out of view. Though Trout himself felt slow down here, at his periphery movement seemed quick and alarming; even the seaweed appeared animate, conscious, breathing. He saw creatures flitting in and out of it—creatures made of seaweed, with long tendriling tails. It was like the world was speeding up while he was slowing down—he belonged less and less to it.

He closed his eyes, and another wave of sleep

almost overcame him. For an absurd moment he felt a desire to remove the mouthpiece for the scuba. He could let himself drown down here, swallow mouthfuls of bitter brackish sea, burn his lungs with salt. His eyes closed again. He was weary. He was weary. Perhaps this was what he'd wanted; this was what he'd come down here for. To sleep, to reside here in darkness in the perpetuity of an underwater night. To shed his human skin and become a creature of seaweed and salt, for his bones to collapse into the seabed like the skeleton of the broken ship.

When his eyes opened, he stared blearily through the dim green light that filtered through the seaweed. He searched for Grunt. Something flicked in, then out, at the edge of his vision, flippered feet past his face. He followed, struggling to stay awake.

CHAPTER TWENTY-SEVEN

The domatia *was in darkness*; Undine's family slept. She let the door click closed behind her, padded barefoot through the flagstone courtyard and across the sandy road to the beach. The moonless night leaked from the sky into the sea and blackness enveloped Undine; only in the village did the occasional light twinkle.

In a half dream she let her clothes fall from her body, onto the sand. Cool night air prickled her skin, raising the hair follicles on her arms and legs, but she was barely aware of these ordinary human responses. Where the pain had struck her before, her body still burned, but this was not ordinary or human; this was magic.

She stepped into the sea, which was neither warm nor cold. The salt and the waves were a salve, soothing the troubled magic within. It sang to the sea and the sea murmured back. Undine closed her eyes and let her own self fade as she listened to the magic's song. She was scarcely aware that she was walking deeper and deeper into the liquid black.

Her feet kicked off the sea floor and she found herself familiarly weightless. The sea held her. She swam downward and felt herself change. The magic took over her body and her body became less solid, less permanent, and more like the sea that surrounded it. Her mind drifted as the magic took hold.

She continued to plunge through the heart of the sea, down far beneath the surface. A light appeared in front of her eyes, and though she'd never seen anything like it, the light was familiar— it felt like home. She didn't hesitate, she didn't stop to think about how her human self would survive so far beneath the sea's surface, she simply swam toward the light, drawn by a power stronger even than her own.

Once upon a time, in the most ancient of lands, Maxine Madden's father had driven an FJ Holden up a mountain, gone for a walk, and disappeared. For a week he had been in limbo, neither dead nor alive, just missing.

For that week, Maxine had pictured him in a landscape much like this one, a kind of nothing place, composed of only the most basic of elements.

In the beginning before light there was chaos. The universe was infinitely dark and infinitely dense. Then there was light and that light was this light: white, pulsating, arrhythmic, prelinguistic. The light that came from chaos, the light that was *chaos.*

Max drew closer to the light, she was an insect, she desired it, she wanted to burn hot and white— to scorch, to scald, to blister; to shine, to blaze, to glory. This was *magic*, this was chaos. This was Maxine's universe, trapped in a bubble of light, or at least it was the key to her universe—or a door. A door, or a window, where she could reach through and rearrange everything. . . .

If he could be found anywhere, her missing one, it would be here in this place. She would tear him from the light, restore him from chaos. And they would laugh, because what was chaos but the mouthpiece for the laughter of the universe? Chaos was nature's capriciousness, where dull, painful things could be rendered absurd and humorous, like an old man's hairpiece on a windy day.

The light dazzled, reflecting off the small scratches on her diving mask. She pulled it off, blinking her eyes open in the salty water. Adjusting the breathing apparatus at her mouth, she entered the underwater room made of light.

• • •

Trout kept the flippers in front of him in sight. His own legs were weary, and the tiredness he had been fighting continued to plague him; his whole brain was lethargic now. His tiredness disoriented him; it took him longer than it should have to realize that whoever he was following wasn't leading him to the boat, but instead back toward the light, the magic that spun with the nervous, pulsing energy of Undine.

It was not Grunt who had led him back to the light. His outstretched hands touched something smooth and hard—he grasped it and examined it in the gloom. It was a diving mask. He let it go; it drifted from him. He watched it and considered returning to the surface. Instead he propelled himself forward, approaching the bubble of magic, for all of a sudden he knew that the diver was Max and that she had fully entered the sphere of light. Why had the magic taken her and not him? He didn't know. But whatever his feelings for her, as twisted and conflicted as they were, he knew he had to help her before the magic swallowed her whole.

Undine was barely Undine anymore. She could hear water, what it sounded like when you were under it, swishing around her ears. Was she under it? Was she still in Greece or was she—could she be—back in the bay? She remembered the light, entering it. Was she nowhere? Was she dreaming? She could not make her thoughts stay together. She drifted . . . she drifted from herself.

She could feel the magic, pulling and tearing at her, as though it had half broken its prison already. And she could feel something else, something like sharp, raking fingernails scratching her skin from the inside. As if someone was trapped inside her, trying to claw their way out. At first she thought it was the magic, that it had become a whole other person inside her, that it had grown fingers and arms and skin and flesh and fear. But then she realized someone really *was* trapped. Not inside her, but inside . . . inside the *magic*, as though trapped inside one cell of her vast brain. The magic was within and without, interior and exterior, over and underlapping.

Undine tried to bring her thoughts together before she drifted again, further from herself, before she disappeared altogether. She saw that she was in an orb of light and inside it with her was a girl, wearing a wet suit and breathing apparatus but no mask. Her blue eyes pierced even the bright aura of light around her.

"Who are you?" Undine asked her.

But the girl didn't answer. She continued to claw and tear at the magic and at Undine. The girl had lost language; she was losing her human-ness.

"You have to go," Undine said. "You're hurting me." Undine thought for a moment and then added, "You're *killing* me."

But it was as if the girl was no longer human. She was muscle, tendon, grasping hand and lidded eye. She was without language, thought, desire; she was barely alive. If she was killing Undine, Undine was also killing her, and Undine had a flash of instant clarity—for one of them to live, the other would have to die.

Half awake, Lou reached into the space beside her, looking for Jasper, who had fallen asleep in her bed. He wasn't there. She opened her eyes and sat up, searching the darkness. There he was, his pale, lean body standing by the window, looking out toward the moonlit sea. He looked so small and frail in the dark, Lou felt a maternal protectiveness swell inside her.

"Jasper, sweetie," said Lou. "Come back to bed. It's sleepy time."

But Jasper didn't turn around.

"Undine's gone," he said, his voice thin and high in the syrupy warm air of the dark room. "Undine's gone into the sea."

Trout circled the light. It was so bright he could not look directly into it. He tried to find a rift, a rupture; he felt blindly with his hands, looking for a way in. Before he had plunged his hand inside it quite easily; now it behaved more like silicon, with a yielding membrane. It undulated at his touch but didn't give way.

Emanating from the bubble he still felt her, now more than ever—Undine, not Max—as though she were almost close enough to touch. *Who's going to die for you?* The phrase echoed in Trout's mind, in his own voice, though he had no idea where it came from.

Suddenly he felt something plunge outward through the bubble's skin. Trout grabbed it—it felt like a human hand—and at that touch he could feel himself shift from his place at the edge of the light to somewhere else entirely, and his mind went white.

And then he saw: a girl on a hillside erupting into a cacophony of butterflies—stones fell and earth crumbled. He saw a narrow laneway and a bald, smooth-skinned man shouting. He was on the steps, he could feel them under his feet, he could taste the air. He saw Jasper, laughing, running, wearing a red jumper. He saw Lou and she was laughing, too, bent double clutching her sides, joy bubbling from her. He saw himself at the bottom of the steps, his face raised and bathed in sunlight. He saw Grunt in a soft snowfall. He looked down at his hand and instead of it being gloved and underwater, it was long-fingered and feminine, and wrapped around it was Prospero's gnarled curling fist. He saw a man's hands on the round globe of Lou's pregnant belly and then Stephen's softly smiling face and crinkled gray eyes. He saw, impossibly, Lou, Stephen, Undine, and *Jasper* walking hand in hand up a beach, a perfect family. Image after image flashed through his mind, like playing cards being flicked onto a table one by one, faster and faster, as if searching for one in particular. And then they stopped, pausing on one moment, one memory. There was Trout, and the green shirt. It was night in the bush at Duncan's party, lights from the dance floor danced around his head. Undine leaned in, and this time their lips touched.

"Undine," the image of Trout said, his lips brushing against hers as he spoke. "Please. I know you're here. Don't let her die. Take me. Take me instead."

Undine's eyes were closed, her mouth pressed harder against his. He felt himself disappearing, descending into that kiss.

With enormous effort, he wrenched himself away. "The girl *is* the magic," Trout said. "But the magic is also the girl. Undine, I beg you. Please."

Anxious and helpless, Grunt searched through the water. Trout had been behind him, but at some point in the forest of kelp, Grunt had lost him.

He surfaced for a moment, and saw the little boat tethered to theirs, bobbing emptily in the sea. It could only be Max; she must have followed them. And now she and Trout were down there and Grunt was not. He plunged back down, looking for them.

He searched through the sea's forest desperately. His hands found something in the weeds—a mask. *Property of the University of Tasmania.* Max's or Trout's? Grunt couldn't tell.

He clasped the mask and swam urgently on through the water, toward the wreck, acutely aware that his tank, which he had used the day before, had less air than Trout's or Max's and that soon— with or without them—he would have to return to the surface.

Lou and Prospero stood on the beach, staring out at the empty sea and the crowded night sky that stretched endlessly above and beyond them. The bright, full moon shone blue-white, so that Lou could see the white caps of the waves. Lou had found Undine's crumpled clothes on the sand, and she held them tightly, as if she could wish Undine back into them.

She had left Jasper at the hotel with Lena. "Leave the boy here," Prospero had said, and Lou had seen he was right, though Jasper had wailed and pulled to escape from Lena's strong grip.

Lou looked back at the hotel for a minute—was Jasper there now? She examined the dark sea again for some sign of Undine emerging.

"Where is she?" she asked Prospero. She wanted to blame him, to rail against him, to beat his weak, frail body with her fists until he lay broken. But she knew this time he was not at fault.

Prospero took her hand, and though her instinct was to recoil, she found his touch surprisingly soothing, and she gripped tighter.

"She's strong," said Prospero. "She's stronger than you think."

"Is she?" asked Lou, and she really wanted to know. "*Is* she?"

Prospero didn't answer, and Lou knew he felt as helpless as she did. Together they watched the black sea and waited.

Undine and the girl stared at each other for a long, silent moment, and then Undine stepped past her.

"You have to leave," said Undine.

But still the girl didn't seem to understand; she butted the light like a moth.

Undine put her hands on the wall of light, and, improbably, she found herself to be touching her own magic inside her. In one motion of great strength she pulled open a rift, screaming in pain—and through her scream she heard Trout cry out. Ocean water flooded in through the opening.

The girl seemed to hesitate, then quickly she dived through the rift. Through the opening, Undine saw another diver, and he saw her. His eyes were concealed by a mask, his face covered. But she knew who it was. She held her hand out to him, through the space in her own magic. She could have pulled him in, or he, her out. He held out his hand—was he offering himself to her? Or was it merely a gesture of good-bye? Their hands almost touched. And then, with a wave of relief, Undine let go and the walls of light descended, separating them, and the light's wound sealed.

She was enclosed by the light, enclosed by the magic, enclosed by her own self. Time here didn't matter. She was outside time, even outside space, she was *between* spaces—she was nowhere. She could drift here, endlessly, a pure form of the magic . . . She could let go of her body, of her self and just . . . *eternal . . . boundless . . . be.*

She could feel herself dissolving. The magic was taking over; the magic was taking her. Her memories, her thoughts—all the things enclosed in the cells of her—dissolved, too, and she let them go: photographs developing, overexposing, vanishing into white.

But then one image floated to the surface and she found she was unwilling to let it go. She fought to hold it, she seized it with all her strength, and as she pulled, the magic pulled back and then the light closed in, it closed in, squeezing and clutching her. And then . . .

And then everything is light, is light and then there is . . .

CHAPTER TWENTY-EIGHT

Trout climbed up, up out of the darkness. He held Max under her arms, pushing her out of the water, and then he broke through the surface into the blinding sun. He reached to his face and tore off his mouthpiece, choking on clear blue air. At first he couldn't see the boat, but within moments Grunt was there, leaning over and hauling first Max and then Trout into its hull.

"What happened down there?" Grunt asked. "I had to come back up, I ran out of air. I couldn't find you. . . ."

But Trout couldn't answer. He opened his mouth,

and suddenly out of him tore a gut-wrenching sob. He leaned over, kneeling on the boat's floor, forehead to the ground, his whole body wracked with crying. Grunt held him, leaned over and held his back, while Max lay, inert and blank and lifeless in the boat's hull.

"She wouldn't take me. She didn't want me. The magic, the sea . . . it was indifferent. . . ." he sobbed, barely coherent. He had offered himself, a sacrifice, a gift, a life for a life, and the sea wouldn't take him. Undine wouldn't take him. He looked up at Grunt. "I thought that was it, what I was meant to do. Last year, when I should have died . . . when Undine used her magic to save me . . ."

Grunt listened. "But it wasn't Undine who pulled you out of the bay. It was her old man. It was Prospero."

"What?"

"He pulled both of us out of the bay; he delivered both of us to safety. I saw him, just before he did it."

"It wasn't . . . it wasn't Undine?"

"No."

Trout wasn't sure why that made a difference, but it did. He hadn't been saved by Undine, by the complexity of her feelings for him. He had just been saved. He didn't owe his life to her, nor had the fish's life replaced his. Prospero had saved him, Undine had made the fish into Trout—they were separate acts and somehow his accountability for the life of that fish dissolved.

"So the fish . . . ?"

"Was just a fish."

". . . was just a fish," Trout repeated, incredulous. "But if I'm not meant to be dead, why does it feel like this? Why is *living* so hard? Why do I feel so . . . empty?"

"Because," Grunt said, laying his coarse hand firmly on Trout's face. "Because. Sometimes that's just the way it feels to live. For all of us."

Trout remembered Max. "We have to get her to shore."

But Grunt was already turning the boat about, steering it toward the shore, towing the empty aluminum dinghy behind. It knocked tinnily against the sailboat, and the sound of it echoed across the surface of the sea.

Trout sat with Max in the boat as Grunt ran up to the house. Max's face was frighteningly still. He thought about what it must have been like for Undine to pull his apparently lifeless body from the bay. He had always thought it was his pain, his private, personal, existential crisis. But now he realized his death did not belong just to him. It also belonged to Undine; it was *her* crisis, her terror, her pain.

Max didn't wake, but her chest rose and fell steadily.

Grunt came back with a blanket for Max, and clothes and a cup of strong, sweet tea for Trout, and they waited for the ambulance.

Still staring at Max, Trout asked Grunt, "Do you love her?"

Grunt looked questioningly at Trout.

"Undine. Do you love her?"

Grunt was silent; he looked up toward the cleft in the dunes, waiting.

It didn't matter anyway, Trout knew. Undine wasn't free to choose Grunt any more than she was free to choose Trout. She could love both of them or neither; the outcome would remain unchanged. She belonged to the magic, and it belonged to her, more than Trout or Grunt ever could. As he tested this thought, he was surprised to find that the pain of it, while it throbbed sharply in his chest, didn't debilitate him.

He looked out at the bay and it seemed changed. The surface no longer looked impenetrable and concealing; instead it was more like a necessary skin, containing and protecting the life within it. The bay was regretful, as if it had lost something essential and precious. The sorrowing angels stood their sentry, looking far out to sea, beyond where human eyes could see. Trout wondered if the bubble of light, and Undine within it, had vanished completely.

Over the head of the dunes came two ambulance officers, a man and a woman; their white and navy uniforms looked clean and orderly as if their whole days weren't filled with disorderly things. They made their way over the beach and stepped through the shallow water to the boat.

They checked Max over carefully and removed the diving apparatus. Trout and Grunt had been reluctant to tamper with her unconscious form, wary of moving her any more than was necessary. The officers unzipped her wet suit and uncovered her chest to examine her—Trout and Grunt both looked discreetly away—then transferred her to the stretcher.

Grunt and Trout walked with the officers to their vehicle.

"Can we get your names?" the man asked.

"Alastair Gray."

"Trevor Montmorency."

The officers glanced at each other awkwardly. The female one said, "You're Trevor? Have you spoken to your family today?"

Trout shook his head.

"You might want to come with us," said the man. "Your mum's been looking for you. You can ring from the ambulance. Now, I need the girl's name, too."

"Maxine Madden."

The man wrote it down and jumped in the back with Max, closing the door.

Trout looked at Grunt, who blinked back at him. He climbed into the front seat of the ambulance and the female officer, who introduced herself as Sharon, got in to drive. Trout watched Grunt as the ambulance pulled away from the house and made its way up Beach Road. Neither of them waved; they just made grim eye contact until the ambulance turned out of view.

He felt numb. As the bay glittered behind him, he wondered what trade he might have made this time. A fish's life for his. What had the bay taken from him in order for Max to be spared?

Sharon made a call and waited. Trout barely registered her side of the conversation, though he heard his name mentioned more than once. His eyes kept closing and he was halfway toward sleep when she passed the phone to him. "Your brother," she said.

"Dan?" he asked the phone.

"No, it's Richard."

"Where are you?"

"At the hospital." Richard's voice cracked. "It's Dad. He's had a heart attack."

Trout's hand went up to his mouth; tears pressed dully at his eyes but didn't surface. "Is he . . . ?"

"He's been in surgery. He hasn't woken up yet."

"I'm on my way. Tell Mum I'll be there soon."

"Take care, little brother."

"You, too."

When Trout replaced the phone, he looked at Sharon. "My dad," he said.

"I know," she said gently. "Tom and I picked him up this morning. He's getting good care, though. The best."

"*You* picked him up this morning?" Trout asked. The synchronicity struck him like a warning bell.

Trout had that hunted feeling again, and the anxiety swelled in him, constricting his breath.

"Yeah. Cover a lot of ground, don't we? We were doing a drop-off in Sorrell when your call came through. Bit of a coincidence though, isn't it? Still, Hobart's a small place. I remember . . ." Sharon's voice filled the car with its soothing, professionally pointless babble about Hobart's brothers and wives and aunts. She required no input from him—rather like a hairdresser or dentist—and he sat back to half listen and half think his own thoughts.

When Sharon explained it like that, it suddenly seemed perfectly logical to Trout. Logic. He breathed. He was a man of logic. He had always believed in it, more strongly than he believed in anything.

Maybe it was time for him to stop being hunted and to stop hunting. Maybe it was time to return to the things he knew: exams, astronomy, Shakespeare. He began to make a deal: if his father could be spared . . . but he stopped. No deals. No magic. It was time to return himself to himself—he'd been holding Trout hostage for too long.

At the hospital Sharon jumped from the ambulance. She pointed a direction to Trout, then instantly forgot him, focusing instead on passing over the motionless Max to the emergency room staff.

The hospital smelled pervasively of cleaning fluid and illness and vegetable soup, but it was a surprisingly soothing smell.

Trout made his way to the reception desk, where they told him his father was in recovery and directed him to the waiting room in which he would find his family.

The first person he saw was Richard and with him his girlfriend, Lucy. She rushed over as soon as she saw Trout and hugged him.

"Oh, you poor things," she said.

Richard hugged him, too. "He's in recovery. They think the operation went well, but we're still waiting for news. He hasn't woken up yet."

Mrs. Montmorency burst into tears when she saw Trout. "We couldn't find you," she said. "I'm so sorry."

"No, Mum," Trout said, holding her to him. It was unusual for them to hug, and he was surprised to find how small and frail she seemed in his arms. "*I'm* sorry. I should have been here."

He looked over his mother's shoulder at Dan, who nodded tightly. His face was white and tense; his hands were clenched fists.

Trout sat next to his mother. Dan sat alone on the other side of the room, under the window. Richard and Lucy held on to each other by the door. The fluorescent lights buzzed overhead; the choking smell of antiseptic, badly brewed coffee, and well-cooked toast filled the air.

"Have you eaten anything?" he asked his mum. He realized he hadn't. His shoulders were stiff and sore from the scuba tank and the oars. His body still hurt from when he had been beaten up, though his mother appeared too distracted to notice his bruises. His empty stomach had an airy, achy feeling.

"There's a cafeteria downstairs," Mrs. Montmorency said absently. "Or a vending machine . . . somewhere. Someone brought me a coffee. . . ." It sat untouched and stone cold by her side.

"I'll find something." But as Trout rose, a doctor entered and he sank to his seat again. His mother stood and so did Dan—Richard and Lucy were already standing—so Trout stood again, feeling faintly ridiculous despite the circumstances.

"At this stage we can safely say that the procedure was successful." Trout felt his mother tremble beside him. "He's awake and asking for all of you, but I'd prefer it if we left most of the visiting until morning. Of course, you may come and see him now," he added to Mrs. Montmorency. She followed him out, glancing back to smile a dazzling relieved smile at her boys, half including Lucy, who she had never cared for in the past.

Richard and Lucy hugged each other and Trout.

Dan sat on a chair, and held his head in shaking hands.

"I feel awful saying this," Trout said, "but I really have to find some food."

"There's a vending machine down the hall," Lucy said. "I can get you something if you like."

"That's okay. I'll go."

Trout selected chicken soup (or what was dubiously labeled "a beverage with the taste of chicken soup") from the hot drinks vending machine. He sipped it and screwed up his face, but persevered. Despite his protesting tastebuds, it felt good to have something warm and at least faintly nourishing in his stomach.

He leaned against the wall, sipping his soup, and found himself wondering about Max, if she was all right. He asked a passing nurse if she knew which room Max was in.

"You really should go to reception. Shouldn't just be wandering the halls. It's a big hospital." But she consulted her chart and was able to direct him down the hall.

As he approached he saw a familiar figure come out of Max's room and walk down the hallway, her back to him. Eliza. He watched her departing back thoughtfully, screwed up his empty cup, and went back to his family.

He found Richard outside, sneaking a cigarette. "I thought you didn't smoke anymore," said Trout.

"Only in times of stress. Lucy got me back onto it, the rotter. And now she's given up, but I can't quite let it go." Richard sighed, as though the cigarettes were some kind of forbidden lover. "Can you keep a secret?"

"I don't know," Trout said, warily. He felt like he'd been keeping so many secrets that they had solidified inside him, turning to hard lumps of coal in his soul.

"It won't be a secret for long," Richard said. "Nature will take care of that."

"All right then," Trout said, still cautious.

Richard beamed, though his brow was slightly furrowed. "Lucy's having a baby."

"You mean she's pregnant? Now?"

"Yes, *now*. That's usually how it works."

"Is that why Dad had a heart attack?"

Richard groaned. "*No*. I haven't told him yet. But thanks for the vote of confidence."

Trout thought about his dad's regret at his sons growing up. "You know what? I think Dad will be happy. Mum will think you should get married, though."

"We might. We've talked about it a bit."

"You don't feel . . . young?"

Richard shrugged. "Sometimes. But I already kind of love it. I don't know. I mean, it's coming now, and . . . we just have to make it work, don't we?"

Trout looked sideways at Richard. "Do you ever think about Undine?"

"No," Richard said, too quickly. Richard met Trout's eyes. "Well, sometimes. But not the way you think. I just wish . . . I wish it had never happened, that's all."

"It's over now." And Trout realized that it really was over, in some way. Or at least it would be.

"I'm sorry."

"Me, too."

They heard a noise behind them and Richard hid his cigarette.

Trout looked up to see Dan's tense face. "Dad's awake. He wants to see you," he said to Trout.

CHAPTER TWENTY-NINE

"*Trout.*"

Mr. Montmorency was pallid and grim-looking—
a kind of gray-white. His eyes seemed sunken. He
was lying down, and his head lolled to face Trout as
he walked in. His lips were loose and droopy, his
normally bright brown eyes faint and dull.

"Trout, come closer."

Trout leaned down and kissed his father's forehead,
a gesture he had not performed since he was about
seven years old.

"Apparently they had trouble finding you this
morning," his dad said. His mouth sounded dry,

and as if his tongue was slightly too big for it.

"Oh, Dad," Trout said, ashamed. "Please don't worry about me. Nothing's wrong with me. Just you get better."

"Pretty sorry state, eh?"

Trout smiled weakly.

"Trout," his dad said, then closed his eyes. With effort he opened them again. "This year . . . something's wrong. You're disappearing."

"I'm not," Trout said. "I promise. I'm back now."

"You're sure?" Mr. Montmorency closed his eyes. He patted his heart. "This old ticker. This machine. I thought I was a goner. I thought I was done for."

"Dad." Trout squeezed his father's hand.

"It's all right. When I was your age, I was so scared of dying. I felt . . ." He stopped and paused for breath. He spoke in spurts, as though each cluster of words hurt him. ". . . cheated by the prospect of it. As I got older . . . the fear for myself just went away . . . but I was so scared of something happening to one of my kids. The day Daniel fell out of the tree outside your bedroom . . . do you remember?"

"I remember."

"But life is resilient."

Trout thought about the baby that Richard and Lucy were having, growing now in darkness, though he seemed to remember reading that even in the womb there are shades of light and dark: light filters through the mother's skin and fat and blood and tissue, the thick membrane and lining of the uterus. Fetuses dream—he read that, too. What do they dream about? Do they dream of light? Is that how birth begins, the adventurer seeking to observe the unknown?

"Yes," Trout agreed. "Life *is* resilient."

"Like me. This morning. A goner. Now here I am."

"Don't wear yourself out, Dad."

Mr. Montmorency coughed and smiled. "Is that your way of telling your old dad to shut up?" His face was grayer than it had been when Trout entered the room.

"Shut up, Dad," Trout said tenderly, and waited till his dad drifted off to sleep.

Out in the corridor he rested his head on the cool wall. He had been a witness, perhaps the only one, to the diminishing health of his father. In those long, lonely nights when only he had been awake to see, should he have observed more closely the ashen skin, the tired voice?

But what could he have done? Could he have held back his father's darkness, any more than he could hold back any night?

He heard someone address him. "Trout."

It was Dan.

"We're taking Mum home. Are you coming?"

"Are you all right?" Trout asked his brother.

Dan nodded, but clearly he wasn't. He looked at the wall. "He nearly died, Trout."

"Oh, Dan." Trout touched his arm. Dan's hand covered his for a fraction of a second.

"All right," said Dan. "That's enough. Stop *touching* me." But he was smiling. "You ready to go?"

"There's something I need to do. I'll walk home."

"Walk!" Dan's face hardened. He crossed his arms. "Where the hell is my car?"

Trout smiled sheepishly.

Trout rapped gently on Max's door. She didn't look up, but stared at the cracks of light coming through the blinds on the window. She was very pale and appeared quite unwell, blue-white like a wintry moon.

"I thought I told you to go away," she said, her voice flat and tired.

"I can leave if you want me to."

Max looked up. "Oh," she said. "It's you." She looked at the window again. She shrugged. "You can stay if you want to."

Trout moved into the room, standing at the end of her bed.

"I know what you think of me." Max still would not meet his eyes. "It doesn't matter anyway. I'm going away."

Trout was surprised. "You're leaving? What about your research? What about . . ."

"The magic?" Max shook her head, her eyes narrow and bitter. "The magic," she said again, spitting the word out as if it were poisoned.

Trout knew then that whatever Max had been looking for, whatever it was that she wanted from the magic, she hadn't found it.

"It isn't to do things," Trout said slowly, as if remembering a long past conversation.

Max nodded, and answered as if in great pain. "I know."

"That's just a side effect."

"You should have left me down there. *She* should have left me down there."

"You would have died."

"It doesn't matter," she said. "Dying doesn't matter."

"Of course it matters," Trout said, angrily. But he wasn't just angry with Max; he was angry with himself. He'd wasted all this time, believing death had some kind of hold over him. Life was . . . it was a kind of responsibility. If he *had* been saved, he owed it to himself, to Prospero who had done the actual saving, and to Undine who had tried, to live. It wasn't much to ask of someone, that they live.

"Then why?" Max said desperately, finally looking in Trout's eyes, searching them for answers. "Why does it feel like this? So flinty and gray and so lonely? Why is *living* so hard?"

"Because," Trout said ruefully, recognizing his own words. "Because. Sometimes that's just the way life feels." He sat down on the edge of Max's bed. "I guess, if you live in darkness long enough, you become a dark thing yourself."

"Are you a dark thing?"

"I thought I was. I thought I was some kind of leftover of the magic, something twisted and strange."

"But you were wrong?"

Trout looked at the light coming through the blinds—glaring white.

"I'm a boy. A man. Made of light. And darkness, shades of darkness."

"I'm sorry I didn't tell you about Eliza."

"So that night in the pub, you planned it? You made it so you would save me and I would trust you?" Trout touched the pale yellow bruise on his face.

Max closed her eyes and nodded.

"I . . . I needed to *reach* you. Quickly. It seems so empty now. But at the time . . . the urgency . . . I *didn't* care about you. I only cared about the magic, that's all. But now . . ."

Trout rested his hand on hers.

"The drugs, too?"

"They were Eliza's idea." Max screwed up her face. "She's kind of . . ."

"She was here, at the hospital. I saw her."

"I didn't tell her anything," Max said, her eyes wide and honest. "I told her . . . I told her you made it all up. That I was wrong. There is no magic."

Trout studied her, not sure whether to believe her or not.

"She's looking for the magic, too?"

"Not really. She's a member of the Chaosphere. And a friend. And kind of a bitch. She helped me find you, that's all. I don't think she ever really believed in the magic anyway."

"But your universe? Your research?"

"It's finished."

"You'd give it all up?" Trout asked softly. "Sacrifice everything you've worked for?"

"For Undine?" Max thought. "Maybe I would. She did save me. But that's not why. And it's not for you either, though if *you* asked, maybe . . ."

"Then why?"

"I know I've done things, horrible things. I don't expect you to forgive me. But I'm not a *bad* person. The magic, it's so . . . living. So fragile. Almost human."

It was a revelation to Trout. "Yes," he agreed, marveling at the idea of it. The girl is the magic but the magic is also the girl—as if the more Undine used it, the more closely tied they became. He had loved the girl, but he'd feared the magic, like it was a monster taking hold of her, making her less human. But now it was as if Undine was tempering the magic, making it *more* so.

"It needs *protecting*." Max sounded surprised at her own compassion. "Besides, I wouldn't be able to use it. It nearly crushed me. It would have if she hadn't . . ."

"So what will you do?"

Max looked away again, staring at the blankness of space in the airy hospital room. "What will I do? I don't know. But whatever it is, it won't be here, in Hobart. There's nothing for me to stay for. Unless . . ." She looked at Trout, who looked quickly away. "I didn't think so," she said softly.

"I have to go," he said apologetically. He stood up.

"I crossed the threshold," said Max. "It wasn't just chaos. It was true chaos. It was discordant, disordered, without structure or form. It tore me from myself." She shivered.

Trout understood. "What descends, ascends. I promise."

"What goes down must come up, you mean?"

Max smiled sorrowfully. "I like it. It has a certain logic to it."

Trout reached out his hand, touched her fingers gently. "Bye, Max."

At the door, he turned back, but Max was already staring at the window again, at the cracks of light coming in through the half-closed blind.

Outside, the late sunlight stretched across the hospital car park, illuminating color with heightened brilliance. Trout looked up at the sun; warm, fragrant air touched his face.

"What was the date today?" he asked a nurse walking past.

She gave him a quizzical stare. "The second of September."

Spring had already happened, and he hadn't even seen it coming. He smiled. Winter was over. He felt it in every bone.

He looked ahead. Grunt was waiting for him,

leaning on the Datsun, which was parked on the busy main road in front of the hospital. Trout raised his hand.

"Hi," he said. "What are you doing here?"

"After you left, Prospero called. It's Undine."

"What about Undine?"

Cars sped by. The world buzzed and sang.

"She's gone."

"Gone?"

Grunt held up his hands, palms facing upward and his fingers open as if she had literally slipped through his grasp. "Gone," he said again, and even the word seemed slippery, as if Grunt couldn't hold on to that, either, the meaning of it. "Gone."

CHAPTER THIRTY

Lou stood in Undine's hotel room. The sheets of the bed were rumpled perfectly in the shape of Undine's body as if she lay there still, but she did not. Instead, where Undine had been was simply an absence of her and the fading breath of the sea.

She glanced out the window. Boats were still searching the sea for Undine as the day's light grew long. She wondered when they would give up and go home. Absently she picked up Undine's jeans from the floor and folded them, smoothing out the creases.

"Louise."

She turned. Prospero stood in the doorway, and though to Lou he had always seemed old, now she really saw his age, as though he was bruised black and blue with it.

"She's gone," said Lou. "She's really gone."

"She's not gone far," said Prospero.

"Do you really believe that? You think . . . you think this is magic? What makes you think she's not somewhere at the bottom of the sea just . . . ordinarily . . . gone?"

"Because I'd know," said Prospero. "And so would you."

"That's what I tell myself," Lou admitted. "That if she was really *dead*"—Lou shuddered—"I would *feel* it. But it's been so long since I let the magic in, maybe I . . ."

Prospero said, "You would know, Louise. It's Undine. She's our daughter. She's *us*: she's made from us, from our bodies and blood and from our history and our magic. We would know."

"Then where is she?"

"I don't know." Prospero shook his head. "But she *will* find her way home. I just hope . . ." Prospero faltered.

"Does she know? About you, I mean?" Lou asked.

He looked away.

"You haven't told her," Lou said quietly.

He shook his head. "I thought there was time. I thought it was mine running out, not hers." He looked at Lou. "I'm sorry I rang you that night, if it was a burden to you. And perhaps you were right, perhaps I should have been honest from the beginning. But I wanted her memories of Greece to be happy, not tainted by grief for a dying father."

Lou watched out the window as the first boats were beginning to return to the pier.

"If she'd known," Lou said quietly, but without accusation, "perhaps she would still be here."

"She'll find her way home," Prospero said again, quietly. "I know she will."

• • •

Trout sat halfway up the steps in the early morning light. The sun was sweet as warmed honey. A crowd of daffodils at his front door nodded cordially to one another.

He closed his eyes and saw in his mind the image of Undine leaving, as though there existed just beyond his reach an infinite moment of leaving. Was there hesitation on her face, as though this time she just might stay?

"Good-bye, Undine," he said, and he could almost taste her on his mouth. He smiled, as only the air and the sky and the passing of birds answered him. "Undine, good-bye."

EPILOGUE

And then there is . . .

Darkness.

And the smell of bacon cooking. She opens her eyes. She's starving.

As if in a dream, she rises from her bed in the attic room of the house on the steps and walks down the stairs in search of breakfast.

She runs her fingers along the wall as she descends. It feels real; the friction of the porous surface of the plaster against her fingertips creates heat on her skin.

Jasper is sitting at the table, drawing. He grins as she approaches. She sees through Lou's open doorway that Lou is still in bed reading the paper.

"Morning!" Lou calls out.

"Morning," Undine falters. She can still smell bacon cooking, hear it crackling in the pan, and in the kitchen someone clutters china cups. She almost knows who it is, but she doesn't let herself believe it.

"Hi, chicken," he greets her. "How do you want your eggs?"

For a moment she can't breathe. She stands frozen to the spot, and then she is falling, falling through the air to get to him.

"Stephen." She is soaking the front of his shirt with tears. "Stephen." She pulls back to look at his face and he looks into hers. "It's you. It's really *you!*"

"Well," he says, baffled. "It's nice to see you, too." And he holds her as long as she needs him to, while the bacon burns and the eggs shrivel and Lou and Jasper look on in bewilderment, and the day outside whirs into life with all the promise and newness of early spring.